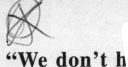

## "We don't h
## I'm your instr

"And none too pleas

"It's part of my job to do whatever comes along. I like my job and I need to keep it."

"Point taken."

He watched, timing his move for the exact moment when she turned to walk away.

If she hadn't been so mad at him for scaring her she might have seen it coming. His arms rose out of the water, circled her hips and brought her plunging backwards into the water.

She came up sputtering in his arms, pounding her fists on his shoulders, angry enough to spit nails.

"You have no right to do that!"

"Sorry, love. I felt sorry for you, standing there in the hot sun when you could have been cooling off in the pool."

"Don't call me that! I'm Miss Grant to you."

"If that's what you want me to call you, Janie, I'll give it a shot. Miss Grant—"

**Jennifer Drew** is a mother-daughter writing team who live in Wisconsin and West Virginia respectively. Before they became partners, Mum was a columnist for an antiques newspaper and her daughter was a journalist and teacher. Both are thrilled to be writing together.

**Recent titles by the same author:**

THE PRINCE AND THE BOGUS BRIDE

# TAMING LUKE

BY
JENNIFER DREW

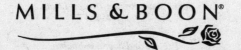

For Erik,
who knew exactly what to do with a 'wild man'
who got out of hand.

### DID YOU PURCHASE THIS BOOK WITHOUT A COVER?

If you did, you should be aware it is **stolen property** as it was reported
*unsold and destroyed* by a retailer. Neither the author nor the publisher
has received any payment for this book.

*All the characters in this book have no existence outside the imagination
of the author, and have no relation whatsoever to anyone bearing the
same name or names. They are not even distantly inspired by any
individual known or unknown to the author, and all the incidents are
pure invention.*

*All Rights Reserved including the right of reproduction in whole or in
part in any form. This edition is published by arrangement with
Harlequin Enterprises II B.V. The text of this publication or any part
thereof may not be reproduced or transmitted in any form or by any
means, electronic or mechanical, including photocopying, recording,
storage in an information retrieval system, or otherwise, without the
written permission of the publisher.*

*This book is sold subject to the condition that it shall not, by way of
trade or otherwise, be lent, resold, hired out or otherwise circulated
without the prior consent of the publisher in any form of binding or
cover other than that in which it is published and without a similar
condition including this condition being imposed on the subsequent
purchaser.*

*MILLS & BOON and MILLS & BOON with the Rose Device
are registered trademarks of the publisher.*

*First published in Great Britain 2000
Harlequin Mills & Boon Limited,
Eton House, 18-24 Paradise Road, Richmond, Surrey TW9 1SR*

© Pamela Hanson and Barbara Andrews 1999

ISBN 0 263 82018 1

*Set in Times Roman 10½ on 12 pt.
01-0009-45403*

*Printed and bound in Spain
by Litografía Rosés, S.A., Barcelona*

# 1

MAYBE SHE was hallucinating.

Jane Grant stopped, rubbed her eyes and let out a low whistle. She wasn't hallucinating. Her always unpredictable boss, Rupert Cox, had added a statue of a Greek god under the cascade of sparkling water in front of the Phoenix headquarters of his sporting goods company.

She'd always loved the high-pressure jet of water, glowing like liquid gold as it caught the early-morning sun and fell into the surrounding pool. A water god was the perfect touch on this August day, his face raised as gleaming water splashed over a body so perfect it made her gasp in admiration. Even from a distance she saw the power in the arms raised to clutch his head and the chiseled grace of the naked torso. If only real men looked like that!

She hurried toward the statue, eager for a closer look before she rushed up to the top-floor offices where she was assistant to the CEO's executive secretary, Miss Polk. Once upon a time she'd wanted to work in a museum surrounded by beautiful things, but little girls had to grow up. It wasn't so bad being a well-paid peon, even if her eccentric boss did like to begin his workday at the crack of dawn, sometimes prompting Miss Polk to ask that Jane come in early, too.

"Oh, no!"

The statue moved.

She froze, hoping she'd only imagined it. Momentary relief that no one had heard her shriek turned to apprehension. There wasn't a security guard in sight, and most employees wouldn't come to work for another hour.

The male version of Galatea, Pygmalion's perfect creation, turned his back to the spray and brushed water from his face with the edges of his hands, then slicked back a long mane of wet hair.

He was taking a shower in Rupert Cox's prized fountain! How could he? Didn't he care if he got into big trouble?

"Oh, this is too much!"

She was too agitated to be afraid of the trespasser. Where did he get the nerve to use a beautiful ornamental fountain as his personal tub? If Mr. Cox saw him… She didn't even want to think of her employer throwing a fit and having another heart attack.

She charged toward the intruder, knowing she had to do something but not sure what.

"You can't do that here!" she shouted from the pavement beside the pool.

He couldn't hear her over the splashing of water.

"Hey, you can't take a shower here!"

Desperate now—as assistant to Mr. Cox's executive secretary she had to take action—she stepped up onto the marble rim of the pool and yelled as loudly as she could.

"You can't use the fountain that way!"

Finally he turned and walked slowly in her direction, as naked as a man could be without getting arrested. The scrap of cloth clinging wetly to his groin was more a pouch than actual underwear; water was dripping from it and trickling down his thighs. His skin was golden tan everywhere she dared look, and water beaded on one chocolate-drop nipple as he raised his arms again to squeeze more water from his hair.

"This fountain belongs to the Cox Corporation. You can't bathe in it!" She tried to sound as intimidating as Miss Polk, but her voice wavered before she could give him an ultimatum.

"I'm not bathing. See, no soap." He held out open palms and looked her over from head to toe, not even trying to be subtle.

She was squirming inside her skin, his steady gaze making her feel as exposed as he was. Worse, she felt like an idiot. It wasn't fair! He was the bare-chested trespasser, and she was doing him a favor by not screaming for help.

He started toward her, moving with unhurried casualness, his long, tanned feet visible now on the slippery aqua tiles lining the bottom of the pool.

"Look, if you're homeless, if you need a place to stay, I have a little money you can have, and a friend of mine volunteers at a mission—"

"Thanks, anyway. A bedroll is enough for me," he said, gesturing toward a knapsack and rumpled sleeping bag on the other side of the pavement.

"You don't understand. You can't camp out on Cox property."

"Oh?" He stopped a few feet away and looked her over again with deep-set blue eyes that shattered the last of her poise.

"You have to leave now."

"Is this Cox a tyrant?" he asked.

"Yes—no…not exactly.…"

She tried to back off the rim of the pool, not realizing how treacherous wet marble could be.

Incredibly, he moved faster than she fell. Instead of plunging forward and landing on her face in the shallow water, she was swept clear of the sharp-edged rim and caught in his powerful wet arms. She instinctively clutched at shoulders as firm and smooth as well-worn saddle leather, then regretted touching him.

"Let go of me!"

"Steady now. Get your footing. The bottom's a bit slick." He had a slight accent, too indistinct to pin down but definitely foreign.

"I can manage."

She tried backing away, but her left foot slipped, thrusting her leg awkwardly between the damp, hairy limbs she was trying to avoid. His thighs closed around hers, preventing a fall but throwing her into a panic.

"Easy does it. I'm not going to hurt you."

Maybe it was his accent; his voice was oddly soothing in a sexy, deep-throated way. For whatever reason, she calmed down for an instant, letting him catch her off guard. He grabbed under her arms and lifted all five foot nine inches of her over the rim of the pool. She stood dumbfounded in the puddle dripping from her legs, shifting uneasily from one soggy foot to the other.

"You can't sleep here, either," she mumbled, looking over her shoulder at his makeshift bed but thinking about his adorable little navel tucked in a nest of fine hairs that thickened at the edge of his practically nonexistent bikini.

Things like this didn't happen to Jane Grant, twenty-six-year-old office worker, substitute mother to her sister, Kim, since their parents' death in a car accident nearly five years ago. Her life was mundane with a capital *M* and would stay that way until Kim finished college three years from now and qualified for a teaching certificate. Jane wasn't the kind of girl who splashed around in fountains with nearly naked men, especially not hunks who made the Greek gods look like sissies.

"It seems I'm guilty of trespassing," he said cheerfully.

She didn't need to look at him to know he was grinning.

"I have to get to work," she said, retreating cautiously.

She glanced down at her neat two-inch bone pumps, pretty sure the discount footwear would dry into stiff, toe-pinching discards. Her cream-colored panty hose were soaked to the knees, but at least her pastel green suit had escaped all but a few splashes on the skirt—and wet handprints where the creature from the company pool had grabbed her.

"Sorry if I delayed you," he said. "Didn't expect anyone to be coming to work so early."

He sounded courteous enough, but she detected a twinge of amusement—maybe even irony—in everything he said. Was he enjoying himself at her expense?

"I'm going into that building," she said, needlessly pointing at the large pseudo-Spanish office complex with light sand-colored walls and ornate cast-iron balconies not intended to be used. "You have approximately three minutes to disappear before security boots you out of here.''

He only smiled more broadly.

''Some of the guards are bigger than you. A lot bigger,'' she added.

His skeptical grin made her feel like a kid yelling threats at a playground bully.

''Thank you for the warning.''

He sauntered over to his gear and bent to roll up the bed.

She didn't want to do it, but her eyes had a will of their own.

She watched.

Good grief! He was a masterpiece! His shoulders and back rippled with muscles under skin as smooth as burnished copper. His waist was lean and his hips narrower than the breadth of his chest. She'd always poked fun at her friends when they rhapsodized over men's behinds, but the Greek god's was world-class: full, round, muscular, undulating just enough as he walked to make her moisten her lips with the tip of her tongue.

And his legs! She was a connoisseur of men's legs. She was tall enough to appreciate height, but most of the men who towered over her had skinny sticks or chunky tree-trunk appendages. The fountain-bather's limbs were perfectly proportioned, gloriously tanned like the rest of him except for shoe lines at the backs of his ankles. It wasn't hard to imagine legs like his wrapped around hers.

She must be losing her mind! Policing the grounds wasn't her job, and Miss Polk treated tardiness as one of the seven deadly sins. She had to go—now. She pictured Miss Polk. The woman she reported to was a walking caricature of a career woman from another era: short and scrawny, but big-busted with unfashionable tortoiseshell glasses and salt-and-pepper hair pulled into a severe bun. She lived in dark suits and probably owned several hundred white blouses, all of which looked as if they had to be ironed. She wore sensible stubby-heeled shoes and sometimes pinned a watch on her lapel to compare the time with that on her large, mannish wristwatch. She intimidated everyone but her immediate and only superior, Rupert Cox. Miss Polk would know how to handle a vagrant who showered under the company fountain.

Jane tried to ignore the squishing in her shoes as she hurried toward the building, not even indulging in another look at the hunk. With a little luck, she might be sent on an errand to the far reaches of the building where she could slip off her pumps and let them dry. Even though she had a title—Assistant to the Executive Secretary—she did any odd job too minor for Miss Polk's personal attention, anything from buying retirement gifts to making travel arrangements. She liked the variety of her tasks, even though she sometimes found Miss Polk's heavy-handed supervision irksome.

But where else could she find a job that paid well enough to support both she and her sister and help with Kim's tuition? Her sister worked hard at a variety of part-time jobs, but as a student her earnings were limited.

When Jane reached the office three minutes late, Miss Polk didn't even glance at her watch. She looked flushed and flustered, making Jane wonder if the Cox Corporation was on the brink of bankruptcy.

In her five years with the company, two as Miss Polk's assistant, she'd never seen her boss pink-cheeked and distracted.

"Oh, yes, Jane, I forgot you were coming in early," the older woman said. "I guess you can busy yourself at your desk for a while."

*Busy herself at her desk?* For this she'd gotten up at an unholy hour, steamed her eyes open in a hot shower, drank three cups of coffee to keep them open and thought of getting a night job as she drove to work? Something was radically wrong, but she knew better than to ply Miss Polk with questions. She didn't want her head to be the first to fall into a basket under a downsizing guillotine.

By ten o'clock Jane had done everything that needed doing and was pretending to reorganize her desk. Her pencils were all razor-sharp, her paper was lined up with military precision and her shoes had stiffened into torture devices. There was nothing left to do but surf the Net on her computer and wonder why Miss Polk kept popping in and out of Mr. Cox's office as though it had a revolving door.

"Jane, Mr. Cox wants to see you in his office," her supervisor said, again slipping through a small opening that didn't allow Jane to see into the opulent interior of the CEO's inner sanctum.

Jane's heart skipped a beat, and she rose to comply with leaden dread. She rarely went into Rupert Cox's private office, and then only to accompany her supervisor and take notes. In fact, weeks might pass without a glimpse of the corporate magnate. He had a private elevator opening into his office and rarely showed himself in the outer office. He never, ever, asked for her by name.

She forced herself to smile, hoping her face wouldn't freeze into an idiotic grin. Looking straight ahead, all she saw was the huge mahogany desk, the surface as smooth and shiny as glass, and the telescope Mr. Cox used to survey the grounds, one of his many eccentric habits.

"Join us over here, please, Jane," his voice boomed.

If Rupert Cox ever lost his financial empire, he could recoup his losses playing movie villains. He had a deep, compelling voice that gave her goose bumps whenever he directly addressed her, which was blessedly seldom.

His office had the floor space of a two-bedroom apartment, one side lavishly furnished with period furniture, including sofas and chairs upholstered in what he called bawdy-house red brocade. There, unceremoniously sprawled on a Victorian love seat, with his feet propped on the surface of a carved and polished ebony table, was the last man she ever expected to see again: the Greek god.

"We won't need you anymore for now, Miss Polk," Cox commanded.

The executive secretary moved slowly toward the door, her whole body stiff with disapproval. Jane wanted to beg the woman not to desert her, but Cox himself was escorting Jane to a chair, his hand firm on her upper arm.

"Jane, I'd like to formally introduce you to my grandson, Luke Stanton-Azrat. Stanton is his father's name. Azrat is a name some African tribe tacked on."

"An honorary name I choose to keep," he said,

standing and acknowledging her with a nod, but staring so intently she thought of X-ray vision.

He was even more dangerously disturbing with clothes than without—not that what he was wearing could be called office attire. His khaki shorts left most of his thighs bare, and he'd apparently ripped the sleeves off a shirt the same color. His feet didn't look slender now in chunky ankle boots with heavy gray socks folded down over the tops. His hair had dried to a sandy-brown with sunbleached streaks of gold. And he seemed taller standing here in the office, at least six-two.

"You're from Africa, then," she said because some comment seemed to be expected from her. What was there to say to a stranger after she'd seen him practically naked?

"I see you've dried off quite well," the grandson said, not responding to her comment. "Sorry to be the cause of your drenching."

"Thank you."

What on earth was she thanking him for?

"Don't be uncomfortable on my account," he said with a sheepish grin as he resumed his seat. "Grandfather saw your valiant effort to eject a savage from his fountain." He gestured at the high-power telescope sitting on a tripod overlooking the front grounds.

"Damn cheeky, Luke," Mr. Cox said with no ill will. In fact, he seemed to be amused by his grandson's prank. "Of course, you'll have to shape up after this. Not act like you're wallowing in some blasted watering hole."

His grandson didn't look intimidated, but Jane felt two inches high with a feather for a backbone.

She was sitting precariously on the edge of an antique chair, the upholstered seat too slippery and rounded to accommodate her bottom in comfort.

His grandson was still examining her with hooded eyes, managing to look totally at home on a piece of furniture designed for a five-foot woman in hoop skirts.

Not for the first time, she wondered why she'd been summoned to the lion's den.

LUKE KNEW what was coming and sympathized with the woman even as he tried to hide his amusement. Judging by her reaction to his early-morning dip, he expected her to go ballistic.

"I'm not a young man," Rupert was saying, sucking in his gut and throwing back his still-broad shoulders in an attempt to belie his statement. "As you know, Jane, I had a heart attack last year, and I've had to give a lot of thought to the possibility of retiring."

Jane. Janie. Luke liked a nice simple name.

"You may also know my only child—my daughter—preceded me in death a few years ago. Now, Jane, Luke is, so to speak, an orphan and my only direct descendant. That also makes him my heir."

Rupert tended to use a person's name a lot when he wanted something. Luke made a mental note of this technique. Even though he had no intention of staying in the States longer than the six weeks he'd rashly promised, he had a deep curiosity about this stranger who was his only living relative.

"I want to be very up front with you, Jane. My daughter eloped to Africa with Peter Stanton very much against my wishes. I had a suitable young man all picked out for her, but she wanted to defy me. The marriage lasted only a very short time, then she returned home for a while and later married a Dutch banker, settling down in Amsterdam. Unfortunately, she wasn't able to have more children.''

Luke felt a tinge of familiar anger. He was glad his mother had left him in Africa, but his father had never completely recovered from her desertion. Luke had loved growing up in rough-and-tumble camps while his engineer father worked in Africa, but Dad had grown increasingly morose and reckless, especially after Luke went to England for his degrees in engineering and began his own career. Heavy drinking and a disregard for his own safety had contributed to the bridge-building accident that took his father's life only a year ago. Luke hadn't sought out his grandfather earlier because it would have been a betrayal of his father's wishes.

Maybe if his father had lived, Luke wouldn't have been curious enough about the grandfather he'd never met to answer the man's summons. And it had been a summons, not an invitation, Luke realized.

He'd said no in seven different languages at least a hundred times, but his grandfather was still determined to make him into a company head. When would Rupert believe he wasn't there for a job and didn't need an inheritance? Maybe when Luke figured out why he'd come to visit a man who sent inappropriate Christmas and birthday gifts to a grandson he didn't even know.

All he'd promised was to stick around for six weeks. He didn't know what the devil Rupert expected to accomplish by throwing this pretty secretary at him. Did the old man really think her perky breasts and ripe pink lips would make him forget Africa? His grandfather wasn't the first big chief to sacrifice a virgin to get his way, but Luke could guarantee it wouldn't work.

Now *there* was an intriguing question: Was she a virgin? Certainly she seemed innocent enough in her short but prim business suit. She was a looker, all right, with hazel-green eyes, creamy skin and sable hair pulled back except for the strands that framed her gorgeous face. Her full lower lip had the soft, swollen look of a woman who's been well kissed, but she hadn't dared look him over in the pool the way an experienced woman would. His guess was she was a sensual woman who didn't know what she wanted—yet.

"I want you to be my grandson's tutor, Jane," Rupert said, finally getting to the point.

"His *what?* Mr. Cox, I don't understand! What can I possibly teach your grandson?"

Luke had to bite his tongue to keep from making a few suggestions that would nullify his grandfather's efforts and let Jane off the hook. His grandfather could certainly be persuasive, but how much of his warmth and charm was genuine? And how serious was his heart condition? Another reason Luke had agreed to come was that he thought it might be his only chance to get to know the man who had so bitterly opposed his parents' marriage. His father had taught him a lot about the world, but not much about himself or the past. Now Rupert was coercing an incredibly beautiful girl into a job she obviously didn't want. Luke just shook his head, wondering if coming at all had been a mistake.

"It's very simple, Jane. Before I hand over the

reins of the company to Luke, he needs to learn how we do things in America. In short, I want you to civilize my grandson. Even though he was educated in England, he's spent too much time in the bush.'' He looked at Luke. ''No more stunts like prancing around naked in the fountain.''

''Not quite naked,'' Luke said mildly.

''But why me? I'm not an etiquette expert.'' She sounded desperate.

''You handled the situation in the pool beautifully. Sent the young rascal scampering for his clothes. I saw it all through my telescope.''

''You give me too much credit! Please, Mr. Cox, I'm really not qualified to—''

''According to Miss Polk, you're very well qualified. I expect you to move up the ladder here. But of course, I also expect you to take on any assignment that comes your way. There's no room for slackers in this organization.''

The threat was so obvious, her face paled. Luke's first instinct was to leap to her defense, but he decided his opinion wouldn't sway a man as determined as Rupert. Luke hadn't been able to convince him he had no interest in running a company that made golf clubs and other toys for adults. He was an engineer and a bridge builder, and damned if he'd get calluses on his butt from sitting in an office all day.

Rupert couldn't change his mind, but the older man was trying hard. He'd even managed, in a weak moment when Luke was still concerned about his grandfather's health, to extract the promise that Luke would take over the company *if* he decided to stay in the country.

No way was that going to happen, not even if Rupert threw a dozen sexy secretaries his way.

"Now, do we understand each other, Jane?"

"Yes, sir."

For a minute Luke thought she'd tell his grandfather where he could put the assignment. She didn't, but who was he to pass judgment? Maybe she really needed the job.

"Splendid, splendid."

Rupert sucked in his gut again and slicked back his full mane of silver hair, reminding Luke of an aging wolf who was still fighting to lead the pack. The man was too accustomed to riding roughshod over people and getting his own way. Old resentments surfaced, but so did regrets. Luke knew he was going to enjoy besting the wily corporation head, but part of him wanted to know more about his long-lost relative, his mother's only living parent.

"Think of *Pygmalion*. You do know that play, don't you, Jane?" Rupert asked.

"The flower girl who was made into a lady by—"

"Yes, yes, that's it," Rupert said. "All you need to do is polish Luke's rough edges, show him how we do things here. You have thirty days, then I have some plans for him. I'll have Miss Polk arrange for you to use my vacation home in Sedona. You'll have an unlimited expense account to spruce him up—buy some decent clothes, among other things."

"You expect me to—"

"Stay in Sedona. No distractions there. This is no forty-hour-a-week assignment, but you'll be extremely well rewarded. You can expect a sizable bonus based on how well you do."

"It's not the money. It's, it's—"

"It's settled. Miss Polk will make the arrangements and answer any questions you may have."

"I'm still going home in six weeks," Luke said under his breath as his grandfather ushered Jane out of his office. It would take more than sacrificing a virgin to put him behind Rupert's desk.

# 2

"TELL ME MORE about this Greek god," Kim insisted, adding her own red tank top to the pile waiting to go into her sister's suitcase.

"He's a wild man! I'd rather try to tame a gorilla."

"He sounds fascinating."

"You know I never wear red," Jane said, noticing the bright garment and seizing on it to change the subject.

"You should. It makes you come alive."

"The last time I checked, I was definitely breathing." She usually wasn't sarcastic, but Kim was treating the whole thing as a lark. It wasn't *her* job hanging by a thread.

"Are you afraid of him?"

Leave it to her sister not to pull any punches.

"No, not afraid, but he's so…so—"

"Masculine? Macho? Untamed?" Kim put the red top into the suitcase along with her own yellow bikini. Jane was too agitated to protest.

"Smug. That's it—smug. You should see his smirk."

"I'd love to. I'll go with you and help."

"There's an idea." Jane considered it, but she'd been a substitute mother too long to let her sister walk into trouble with her. "Unfortunately, you have classes starting pretty soon and a new job at the Steak House.''

''My loss! How long do you expect to be gone?''

''I have thirty days to do the job.''

''You'll be staying alone with Jungle Boy for a whole month?''

''No! No, no, no! Miss Polk guaranteed we wouldn't be the only ones there. A couple live there and take care of the place, and company execs are scheduled to come in two- and three-day shifts to teach him the business. I'll just be his…''

''Nanny?''

Jane laughed for the first time since Rupert Cox had dropped the bombshell on her.

''That's as good a title as any. I have to ride herd on a man who showers in public fountains.''

''Wish I'd seen that.''

''Well, I wish I hadn't. Then I wouldn't be in this mess.''

Also, she wouldn't be speculating how he kept the little pouch from falling off. Maybe it was some trick he'd learned in Africa.

''Maybe you can finish in less time,'' Kim suggested optimistically. ''Although I don't think I'd want to. What's so terrible about staying in Mr. Cox's fancy Sedona hideaway?''

''Being blackmailed into it.''

She couldn't sacrifice her career to get out of the assignment. It was that simple. And complicated. Her chances of getting another job as good as the one she had were nil if Cox fired her. And she'd promised her mother, in her heart, that she'd take care of Kim. That meant helping with tuition as well as paying the rent, and her salary and benefits at the Cox Corporation were excellent for someone with only a two-year associate's degree in business.

"Look at it as an opportunity to meet new people—male people especially. Chances are there'll be a whole parade of neat guys coming to the house," Kim said.

Kim's curly-haired, dimpled cuteness was a magnet to the opposite sex, and she was always urging her big sister to be more aggressive, to go after men who attracted her, and to date more to get into circulation.

"Button-down business types, the same ones I see every day at work."

Even talking to her sister, Jane couldn't stop thinking about bronzed skin glowing in the morning sun and muscles rippling under golden spray. She knew why her dating life was so abysmal. She'd always been intrigued by adventurous, bigger-than-life men who intimidated her so much she shied away. She wasn't the kind of woman who rode on the back of a motorcycle or hung around dives to attract rodeo riders, but pale-skinned business types bored her.

"I can understand why you're a charter member of the born-again virgins," Kim teased. "The only man you ever slept with was Bryan, and he was more interested in himself than he was in you."

Jane tossed Mr. Hopper, her shabby stuffed kangaroo, at her sister and missed. Kim sure had her number: The small group of friends she hung with did spend a lot of time griping about their practically nonexistent sex lives and wondering if they'd ever sleep with a real he-man—or even have a decent first date.

Being single was complicated enough without putting her personal life on hold to civilize a drop-dead gorgeous wild man.

"Anyway, no one can blame you if the guy is totally incorrigible."

"Failure is not an option," she said, quoting Miss Polk who frequently repeated Cox's favorite trite maxim.

"What have you got to lose?" Kim asked.

"My job," Jane said dryly.

"Let me get this straight. You're off to spend a month tutoring a virile hunk who oozes sexuality from every pore. He has a body worth giving up chocolate for and a dreamy face, but you don't want to go because he's too self-confident."

"Smug and cocky."

"Because he plays by his own rules, not anyone else's?"

"He thinks he can do whatever he wants regardless of how other people feel about it."

"Are you sure you're not just scared silly of having a close encounter of the romantic kind?"

"Don't you think about anything but men?" Jane asked.

She knew her question was unfair. Kim worked hard and got excellent grades. But Jane wasn't in the mood to be analyzed by her cheeky little sister. And she wasn't reassured by Kim's sly smile.

THE SLEEK RED leased Ferrari was a bit of all right, making Luke smile to himself as he negotiated the switchback roads to Sedona with the skilled touch of a professional race driver. In fact, he'd driven in a few races but didn't like the lifestyle of a pro: constantly traveling and staying in crowded, constraining cities. He belonged in Africa, doing what his father had done. No doubt his grandfather had learned about his love for fast cars by having him investigated. It was one more lure to bring him into his grandfather's business.

"It won't work, Rupert," he said aloud, wishing he hadn't felt compelled to come to Arizona to meet his only relative. True, he felt a wary fascination, wondering how much of his own character came from his maternal grandfather, but it was much too late to form any kind of bond.

The elder man had promised, as a condition of Luke prolonging his visit, not to interfere if he decided to leave in six weeks. He was going back to Africa to do what he loved best, and a company of mercenaries wouldn't be able to drag him back into his grandfather's net.

"Sly old devil," he said with a trace of affection.

Not only had he found his grandfather looking robust in spite of his heart problem, but Luke seriously doubted the man would ever willingly give up the power of his position as CEO. He might make his grandson a figurehead, but he'd still be there, pulling strings. It didn't matter. Luke had his life mapped out, and it didn't include Rupert's company.

Jane was a wrinkle he hadn't expected, though. Was she in on the plan or had Rupert decided to use her on the spur of the moment? Him and his bloody spyglass!

He wouldn't put it past the old reprobate to find the sexiest woman around and disguise her as a prim-and-proper career girl. Who better to get inside his head and report back to Rupert?

No, she was probably just what she seemed: an

employee roped into teaching him some manners—
American-style manners, that is. She hadn't been acting when she ordered him out of the fountain. He'd
shocked the pants off her—or rather, he wished he
had. He wouldn't mind cavorting on the front lawn
or anywhere else with her. She was the genuine ar-
ticle, all right, and too gorgeous for her own good—
or his.

He was still disappointed that she'd insisted on
driving her own car instead of riding to Sedona with
him. Looks aside, he wanted to pump her about his
grandfather, and it sounded as though there would be
lots of watching eyes and curious ears when he got
to the house.

He expected plush digs, but the red rocks of Sedona were so spectacular under the hot August sun,
he wouldn't mind camping out with his bedroll. The
landscape was a deep orange-red like burning coals,
but the town itself was plagued with tourists who
didn't have enough sense to take a siesta on such a
hot afternoon.

Just off Highway 89-A, he approached his grandfather's hideaway. The house had adobe walls and
heavy Spanish tiles on the roof, but it also had a
security gate with a uniformed guard on duty.

"Is Miss Grant here yet?" Luke asked, stopping
even though the guard had motioned him ahead as
soon as he recognized the car.

"Yes, sir. She got here a couple of hours ago driving a white compact—"

"Much obliged," Luke said, not needing a full
report.

She was expecting a wild man. He decided not to
disappoint her. It wasn't going to be easy, treating

her like a primary-school teacher, especially since he'd spent his early years being tutored in construction camps, but the last thing he needed was to get involved.

''Bloody hell,'' he said, knowing how complicated his stay would be if he let himself do any of the things he could so easily imagine doing with Miss Jane Grant. A man could make some silly decisions with those long, shapely legs wrapped around him. It was much safer to make sure she wouldn't want anything to do with him.

Leaving the car in the circular driveway, he quietly eased the door shut, leaving his socks and shoes in the boot along with his shirt, wallet and watch. He used the magnetized holder to hide the keys under the fender. He debated whether to strip off his walking shorts, but settled for pushing them low on his hips.

He'd asked Polk enough questions about the place to know the lay of the land. Nice old girl, Polk, he thought, idly wondering whether her loyalty to Granddad went beyond the office. Rupert must have some hold on her, the way she scampered around, knocking herself out for the old man's every whim. Of course, there was no understanding females. If he'd read Jane's eyes right, she wanted to tell Rupert to go soak his head in his own pool.

But she was here, ordered to undo the habits of years spent in road-building camps, running with native kids and generally raising hell when his father was too busy to pay attention, which had been most of the time.

''Good luck, honey.'' He grinned, thoroughly enjoying himself for the first time since coming to the States.

He made his way barefoot to the rear of the sprawling adobe house, pleased to see that Rupert had landscaped the place with rocks and cacti instead of trying to transform the desert into a phony version of Versailles. The environmentalists in Phoenix were probably ready to lynch him for his water-wasting fountain.

He found Jane doing exactly what any wage slave chained to a desk most of the time would do when suddenly thrown into the lap of luxury: idling by the pool.

Even at four o'clock, the sun was blistering hot, and she had sense enough to stretch out on a lounger shaded by a big umbrella. He stopped, still concealed by the corner of the house, and decided his memory hadn't played tricks on him. She was stunning.

Better still, she was alone and sprawled out without artifice: a modern-day Eve in a bright yellow bikini, one knee drawn up and serving as a prop for a magazine she was reading.

He'd recognize her legs anywhere: long, smooth, shapely. He speculated how it would feel to rub sunscreen from her cute little toes to the sleek fullness of her thighs, parted now with only a narrow bit of cloth between them that sparked his imagination like a torch set to dry kindling. Which was why he needed to make sure she'd never let him, even if it meant scaring her a little with his wild ways.

His luck couldn't be better. She looked heavy-lidded and languid, only moments from falling asleep. What he really wanted to do was wait until the magazine fell, a sign she'd lapsed into dreams, and wake her with a kiss.

Bad idea! Too personal. He didn't want her to scurry back to Phoenix. The next tutor his grandfather sent might not be so much to his liking.

He let out a fiendish howl.

It was a war whoop owing more to Native Americans than Zulu warriors, but it definitely got her attention.

She shrieked.

He ran toward her, but veered off at the last second, plunging feetfirst into the pool.

He swam, slicing through the tepid water with powerful strokes, performing for her but immensely enjoying every lap for the release it gave him. Rupert had maneuvered him into a six-week stay, hoping to entice him into making it permanent. The best way to get through his "etiquette" lessons was to treat them as a game, he decided, feeling less constrained than he had in Phoenix.

After ten fast laps, he looked over to the concrete apron of the pool and saw what he'd hoped to see: slender ankles and shapely calves.

"You're not funny!" she said, bending forward so her words carried to him loud and clear. "You startled me, but it was a trick a ten-year-old would pull. If you think I'm going to run back to Phoenix because of your silly stunts, you're in for a surprise, Mr. Stanton-Azrat."

He was impressed. She remembered the name he'd made up to seem more alien to his grandfather. He wondered if she'd noticed any similarity between his so-called tribal name and a rodent's behind.

Swimming over to tread water near her feet, he looked up and grinned guilelessly.

"Sorry I acted like a crazed wildebeest scenting water. I just had to go for it."

"Do wildebeest shriek like a bad movie version of Geronimo?"

She was sharp, this one, but he had a few more tricks up his pant leg.

"Join me," he invited.

"No, thanks."

"Our whole relationship is water-based."

"We don't have a relationship. I'm your instructor."

"And none too pleased about it," he surmised.

"It's part of my job to do whatever comes along. I like my job, and I need to keep it."

"Point taken."

He watched, timing his move for the exact moment when she turned to walk away.

If she hadn't been so mad at him for scaring her, she might have seen it coming. His arms rose out of the water, circled her hips and brought her plunging backward into the water.

She came up sputtering in his arms, pounding her fists on his shoulders, angry enough to spit nails.

"You have no right to do that!"

"Sorry, love. I felt sorry for you, standing there in the hot sun, when you could be cooling off in the pool."

"Don't call me that! I'm Miss Grant to you."

"If that's what you want me to call you, Janie, I'll give it a shot. Miss Grant—"

She splashed hard, sending a wave of water breaking over his head before remembering he was a modern-day Poseidon. Niagara Falls could come rushing down on his head, and he wouldn't care.

"Don't start what you can't finish, Janie."

He dived, and she tried to climb out of the pool, managing to get her arms and one knee over the edge before he struck.

She expected to be pulled back and ducked. Instead, he pulled himself up beside her, pinned her hips down with his arm, lifted her leg beside the other, and kissed the back of her knee. Not once or twice, but repeatedly. She squirmed and squealed until she realized that was exactly what he wanted. He didn't stop until she stopped struggling.

"My favorite flavor—coconut oil." He rose effortlessly and offered her his hand.

There was no graceful way to get from her stomach to her feet. She ignored his hand and scampered to her hands and knees, outraged when he put his arm around her waist and lifted her to a standing position.

"Don't ever do that again!"

"Help you up?"

"Half drown me! Fondle me!"

"I suppose I should've asked if you can swim, but I don't understand the fondling part."

"Oh, yes you do! You—"

"Just being playful, love. No offense intended."

"Don't let it happen again. And don't call me love!"

Luke watched her stalk to the house and disappear through the sliding glass door that opened onto the pool area. What the devil was he going to do with her for a month?

"Seduce her, you idiot," he said aloud, even as his inner voice vehemently warned against it.

Not that he wasn't prepared to. When he went back to working with a construction crew in Africa, the opportunity for fooling around would be rarer than unicorn horns. He had promised himself to have some fun on this jaunt his grandfather had suckered him into making. But Jane was a nice girl—pretty but no party girl. He didn't want any emotional ties to confuse him into staying a day longer than he'd promised himself. And he didn't want to leave any broken hearts behind, a problem that had caused him some complications during his brief stint as a race car driver.

He should just ignore her, but there wasn't much chance of that if she made more appearances in that yellow bikini. He was going to lose some sleep, remembering the way the narrow strips of cloth clung wetly to her spectacular breasts and cute bottom. Plus, it was her duty to civilize him, whatever she thought that meant.

There was only one way to play it safe—to play the part of Tarzan.

# 3

HER NAVY DRESS was missing! Jane searched the clothes the housekeeper had hung in the closet, but it was obvious Kim had slipped it out of the garment bag when she wasn't looking.

Jane loved that dress, even if her sister did call it the date dampener. Now, when she really needed something high-necked, loose-fitting and long, she was staring at Kim's white halter dress, a shorter, skimpier version of a movie-star classic.

"That little sneak," Jane muttered, but it wasn't her sister's wardrobe games that had her two seconds away from bolting.

How on earth could she have any influence on a man so rambunctious and uninhibited and sexy and—

Her cheeks got hot just thinking of lying on the hard wet concrete while a man she barely knew had kissed the backs of her knees.

He was a wild man! And for the next month he was *her* wild man unless she wanted to hit the unemployment line—not exactly an attractive option.

She fumed at the unfairness of being drafted as keeper to her boss's renegade relative. How was she going to get through this?

"By not playing Luke Stanton-Azrat's game," she

told herself with quiet determination, yanking a pair
of beige linen slacks from a hanger.

At least Kim had let her bring a bulky white cotton
cardigan for cool nights. Buttoned to the neck over
a tank top, it would send a message as well as the
navy dress—or even better since it would be obvious
she was only wearing it on such a hot night to dis-
courage his even hotter intentions.

LUKE WANDERED through the downstairs rooms, admiring the house a little more than he wanted to admit. He liked the rough plastered wall tinted the color
of desert sand, the gleaming hardwood floors and the
Navajo rugs in black, red, yellow and turquoise.
There were giant earthenware pots with broad-leaved
plants, black leather couches and chairs, comfortably
indented from long use, and heavy carved wooden
tables with lamps and odd bits that looked like prized
possessions, not some decorator's arty idea of accessories. The caretaker's wife, Wilma, kept everything
polished like a new sports car, but the place still
managed to look as though a man enjoyed living
here.

He slumped down in an overstuffed chair and let
one bare leg hang over an arm, wondering how much
longer it would be before his own personal Ms. Manners came down the iron spiral stairs. Had he over-
done the wild-man bit? He hadn't meant to scare
her—just put a comfortable amount of space between
them. Who knew a little kiss on the back of her knee
would taste like a tropical drink and have the impact
of a stick of dynamite?

He waited, wondering what he'd do if she didn't

show. His first impulse was to carry a dinner tray to her room and apologize.

Nope, too civilized. Better to figure out a way to induce her to come down.

He came up blank, but it didn't matter. The soft click of heels carried down to him. Jane slowly descended the open stairway, hanging on to the railing and keeping her eyes on the steps.

For several heart-stopping moments his eyes followed her progress, taking in the grace of her movements and the way her dark sable hair framed her face. As for her sensational legs, he could only remember them as he'd seen them at the pool. She'd wrapped herself up like a mummy, swathed in bulky clothes from neck to ankles.

"Aren't you going to be too warm in that sweater?" He rose slowly and stood by the chair, wondering how close she'd dare get to him.

"Not at all." Her airy tone didn't fool him. "It'll get cool after the sun goes down."

"That won't be for several hours. You must be planning to linger a long time over dinner." He did enjoy baiting her, not that he thought it was especially laudable.

"Hardly." Her tone brought the temperature down a few degrees. "Is that your idea of dressing for dinner?"

"This is the only coat I brought. Sorry about the wrinkles." He pretended to examine the many creases in his white linen jacket.

"I meant the trousers you're *not* wearing. Do you always wear those…things?"

She was looking a little pink in the cheeks.

"You don't like 'em?" He hitched his thumbs into

the waistband of the old bush shorts he'd hacked shorter with his Swiss army knife just for this occasion.

"They're inappropriate." She was staring over his left shoulder, feigning indifference.

*I don't think so, love,* he thought with a trace of genuine amusement.

"I'm wearing a tie." He tried to sound penitent, holding out the tip of the old striped school tie he'd worn as a kid.

"Most men wear one with a shirt," she pointed out.

*What am I letting him do to me?* she asked herself. She sounded like a critical old maid. Why should she care if he looked like a cartoon wild man? All she had to do was ignore him as much as possible for six weeks—forty-two days. How long was that in hours? Minutes?

"I'm not most men, Jane."

Was that a threat or a warning she heard in his voice? Neither was necessary. She was as wary of him as she would be a tiger that escaped from the zoo. Only in this case, Rupert Cox had made her a very unwilling animal trainer.

"If you two would like to go out to the patio, dinner is all ready," Mrs. Horning said from a doorway on the far side of the room.

"You're a sweetheart, Wilma. I'm so hungry, I could eat half a rhino," Luke said, basking in the approval radiating from the housekeeper.

Jane crossed the caretaker's wife off her very short list of potential allies. Would her husband, Willard, be taken in by Luke's rakish charm, too? Jane had the uncomfortable feeling Luke was playing a game, and she didn't know the rules.

Jane led the way to the recreation room, past the ornate antique billiard table, and through the sliding glass door to the pool area.

"Not this patio, Janie," Luke said, stepping out beside her. "Here, follow me. I had Wilma set the table on the west patio."

"I'd rather you didn't call me that."

"Whatever you like, love. If it's Miss Grant you want, it's Miss Grant you'll get."

"Just plain Jane will be fine."

Even in her sensible inch-and-a-half heels, she was hard-pressed to keep up with his long, lanky strides. And didn't she feel awkward, trailing behind a man who was all legs from the hem of his rumpled jacket to the strap of his sandals! She nearly collided with him when he turned abruptly.

"Plain Jane won't do at all," he said, deliberately twisting her meaning. "Pretty Jane, maybe, or Pouty Jane."

"I'm not pouty!" She automatically covered her lips with two fingers, self-conscious because she did have a habit of pursing her lips when she was thinking hard.

"You're not put out about Rupert making you my guardian?"

She hesitated. "It is unfair. I work hard being at Miss Polk's beck and call. There's no reason for me to be here."

"Me, neither." He grinned and shrugged his shoulders. "We're both dancing to the same tune."

"Not quite. I'm just trying to hang on to my job

until my sister finishes college. You'll take over the company someday."

"It'll never happen. Come on, let's find our dinner, and you can tell me about the pretty sister you left at home."

He put an arm around her shoulders and guided her along a path of round, ruddy-colored tiles. She stiffened under his touch, even though her bulky knit sweater made it as impersonal as a handshake.

The sun was still a fiery orb in the sky, affording no letup in the summer heat. Who knew cotton could be so warm?

When they rounded the corner to the west end of the big stucco house, she could see where the plateau dropped off sharply, allowing an unobstructed view of the famous red rocks of Sedona. It seemed more like a movie setting than real life.

The patio itself had just enough space for a small redwood table shaded by a green-and-gray-striped umbrella. Sitting knee-to-knee, four people could share the table, but Jane felt crowded when Luke seated her on a heavy wooden chair with bright flowered cushions and took his place across from her. His knee brushed hers when he slid the chair close to the table, and his mumbled, "Sorry," did nothing to relax her.

Their places were set with an intimidating number of gleaming silver forks and heavy geometric-patterned china dishes in shades of turquoise and orange. The table was covered by a pale beige linen cloth, with the matching napkins monogrammed *R.C.* A slender-lipped bottle was sitting in a silver cooler filled with ice.

"Wine with a cork," Luke mused, picking up a

corkscrew opener and examining the mechanism. "My guess is, I'm supposed to decant and pour."

If he knew enough to do that, why did he need etiquette lessons from her? Now, if he'd cracked the bottle across the table and taken a swig, she could offer some useful advice—like try not to cut yourself on the jagged edge.

Instead, she refrained from commenting and put the elegant linen napkin on her lap, forgetting to shake it open. Luke stood and tackled the cork, his narrow tie only partially covering a golden-haired, deeply tanned chest. In the wardrobe department, she decided he definitely needed help!

She didn't know where to focus her eyes. Fortunately, Willard pushed through the door at the end of the house, carrying a silver tray.

"Fresh prawns," he said cheerfully. "My wife won't tolerate skimpy frozen shrimp."

"Looks first-rate," Luke said, admiring the big pink prawns served in a crystal dish set in a larger dish of crushed ice.

"Has to be for Mr. Cox," Willard agreed, resting his hands on the front of the white apron covering his rotund, Santa-style belly.

"Very nice, thank you," Jane agreed, a little miffed because Luke was much more at ease with servants and fancy dining than she was. What on earth was she supposed to teach him?

She felt more and more like part of a plot to keep Rupert's grandson entertained.

Worse, she was hot enough for spontaneous combustion. Her face had to be pinker than the prawns, and the sweater was sticking to her shoulder blades like a wet rug. She tried to push up her sleeves inconspicuously as Willard was leaving, but Luke was too sharp-eyed.

"Are you sure you don't want to slip out of that sweater, Janie? Looks to me like we're about three hours from a cooldown."

He grabbed a giant prawn with his fingers, dunked it in spicy red sauce and made it disappear, tail and all, in one big bite.

She picked up the delicate silver cocktail fork at the outer end of the lineup of flatware on her left and tapped it lightly on the edge of the ice dish. He ignored her subtle hint, stuffing a second prawn in his mouth and chewing with gusto while she watched, fork suspended, as his lips moved without restraint.

"Try one," he invited, pushing the tail out of his mouth with the tip of his tongue and planting it beside the first in the mound of ice.

"Don't tell me you don't use forks in Africa!"

"Depends on whether I'm feasting on grubs from under a fallen log or dining with a politico who needs softening up to grant the right permits."

She dropped the fork, wondering whether she was going to faint from heat or squeamishness.

"Only pulling your leg, Janie."

He stood quickly, worried he'd gone too far this time. Either she was shocked silly by the thought of eating grubs, which he had tried and found not especially to his liking, or she had heat prostration from bundling up like an Arctic explorer.

"Here, have a drink. You don't look so good."

He stood, picked up her untasted wine and held it against her lips until she downed a few good swallows.

"That's enough!"

No thanks there.

"You're burning up," he said, touching her cheek with the backs of his fingers. "You'd better peel the sweater off before you pass out. It's hotter than I expected when I told Wilma we'd eat outside."

Stepping behind her, he reached down and undid the row of pearly buttons on her cardigan. She wasn't, both to his relief and disappointment, wearing one of those lacy little brassieres with tantalizing peepholes. A tank top was sticking to her like a second skin, damply outlining the lushness of her breasts. She was a sight to give a man an appetite, and not for dinner.

"Don't do that!" she protested when the deed was already done, pushing his hands away and wrapping the sweater around her like protective armor.

"Just trying to help." He moved into her range of vision and held out his hands palms up, trying to show his good intentions. "I thought for a minute you were going to pass out."

"I'm fine—just a little dehydrated. All I need is some water."

Still holding the sweater shut with one hand, she grabbed a water goblet and drank, noisily swallowing until she drained it.

"Seems we have company," he said, catching a glimpse of a little green creature scurrying around the rear legs of his chair.

The lizard was fast, but Luke was faster. He reached down and captured it by the tail, exhibiting his prize on his palm with the delight of a schoolboy tormenting his teacher.

"He's a cute one," he chuckled, holding it closer to her.

Her little shriek was soft but satisfying.

"He won't hurt you. With all this food, we can spare him a little nibble."

He retrieved one of the prawn tails and laid it on the ground along with the lizard, but the beastie scurried away, too terrified to investigate the treat.

"If you think you're going to get rid of me with dumb stunts…"

He sat down, leaving the chair some distance from the table so he could stretch his legs and lean back comfortably.

"Is that what you think I'm trying to do?"

Putting space between them was good; scaring her off wasn't. It occurred to him that if Jane bolted, Rupert might send Miss Polk to take her place, and he didn't think the iron maiden would be nearly as entertaining.

"Either that or you're naturally boorish."

"Ouch, that hurts," he complained. Oddly enough it did. "Will you take off that Arctic survival wear, relax and enjoy a nice dinner if I promise to behave?"

"Depends on what your idea of behaving is."

"I'll begin by apologizing for the bit at the pool."

"That's a start."

He noticed she wasn't discarding the sweater.

"I'll call you Miss Grant and use every fork in the lineup."

"Oh, finish your prawns," she said with an exasperated sigh.

He hid a smile behind his napkin when she slipped her arms out of the sweater and let it bunch up behind her rigid back. Except for an occasional glance at her chest, he got through the rest of the dinner in good form.

Their conversation revealed that they had one thing in common: They were both orphans. Jane talked willingly enough about her sister, but by the time they finished off the meal with fresh raspberries in a swirl of chocolate sauce, he was pretty sure the only layer she'd peeled off was the sweater. Without being obvious, she was keeping him at arm's length, telling him only things she would tell any stranger. There was more to her than he could begin to guess, but it was probably best if he didn't probe for soft spots.

"Now what?" he asked after Wilma carted off the last of the meal, leaving them with snifters of brandy she was ignoring. "Miss Polk was clear that I get my orders from you. What's on the docket for tomorrow?"

"A little shopping trip."

"I don't shop." That was one piece of nonsense he wanted to squelch right away. "Buy whatever you like. While you do, I'm going to do some hiking, take a look around."

"You have to shop."

Half a bottle of wine had certainly stiffened her spine, but the resolution on her face only made her more delectable. Her tank top had dried, but that did nothing to diminish the appeal of her tantalizing breasts.

"I don't think so," he said firmly. "No shopping."

If she knew him better, she'd know it was time to sound the retreat. Or maybe she had more grit than sense.

"You can't wear jungle-boy outfits to all the meetings on your agenda. Miss Polk has you scheduled—"

"Jungle *boy?*"

"You know what I mean."

"Don't make the mistake of thinking you're my nanny," he said with real seriousness.

"I was given an assignment," she said stiffly. "I don't want it, but I can't afford to lose my job. If you're going to thwart me—"

"Not thwart," he said in a mellower voice. "I just don't shop."

"I can't buy clothes for you. You'll have to be measured—consulted."

"You've consulted me. I like to be comfortable—period."

"Please don't do this to me!" She grabbed the brandy snifter with both hands and tipped it to her mouth.

"It's strong," he started to warn her.

He'd suspected she was no drinker, and her sputtering cough confirmed it. He thought of putting her over his shoulder and patting her like a baby, but his saner self won out. He watched while she gulped water, wishing he wasn't so fascinated by the bobbing of her breasts.

"This is the worst night of my life!" she wailed theatrically.

It could get worse, he thought, beginning to wish she'd put the sweater back on.

"Maybe we can make a deal," he offered, against his own better judgment.

"What kind of deal?" Her words were muffled by the napkin she was pressing against her full pink lips.

"I'll go shopping if…"

He tried to think of something so outrageous, she'd be sure to turn him down. It was going to be a long six weeks if he let her lead him around like a puppy on a leash. Rupert's plans be damned! He wanted to go camping in the mountains while he had the chance to see some of America's Southwest. He didn't expect to ever return to the region.

"If what?" She sounded more skeptical than hopeful—with good reason.

"If you tuck me in." He wasn't sure why he came up with that, but he expected it to be enough to scare her off.

"You mean…" She looked as if she'd just swallowed that little lizard and didn't know what to do about it.

"A proper tuck-in. The kind any good nanny does, since you seem to fancy yourself one. Fluff my pillow, check the covers, tell me a bedtime story."

"You're being ridiculous!"

"Oh, I have to warn you. I never wear jammies. Here's my proposition—I'll go to one store for one tuck."

"Only one shop?"

She couldn't seriously be considering his challenge! No woman alive would be content going into just one clothing store.

"I won't budge on that—only one. And the tuck is done when I say it is."

She sat statue-still. He'd expected her to storm off, maybe dash the last bit of brandy in his face. She was making him edgy—and it took a lot to put him off balance.

"Done."

"You agree to my offer?" He'd misread her and didn't much like it.

"Yes."

"And I'll only go to one shop—one."

"Yes, I understand the concept of one. What time will you be retiring, Master Luke?"

"Let's see." Every instinct he had told him to back down, cancel this nonsense before he outfoxed himself. "I'd like to finish unpacking my gear, check out the news on the telly, get undressed—you wouldn't count that as part of the tuck and help me, would you?"

"It's not part of the tuck. Tell me a time." Her tone was cold enough to give a man frostbite.

"Eleven will do nicely," he said.

She glided away without another word while he sat twirling his brandy snifter and wishing he'd gone straight to Swaziland after his last job instead of satisfying his curiosity about his grandfather. Building a few railroad bridges seemed like a cinch compared to outguessing a woman. Of course, there was always the hope she might change her mind.

Yes, that was probably her strategy: get him all lathered up, then pull a no-show.

He sat brooding for a long time, not enchanted by sunset on the red rocks of Sedona and definitely not looking forward to eleven o'clock. Why had he made such a ridiculous offer?

"You expected her to turn it down, that's why," he muttered, idly wondering what she'd wear to tuck him in.

The more he thought about it, the more likely it seemed she wouldn't come, so he relaxed.

A little.

# 4

HE WAS TRYING to get rid of her.

It was the only possible explanation.

Jane paced the small balcony outside her bedroom window, turning every seven steps when she ran out of space. She felt like some poor squirrel trapped on one of those diabolical miniature treadmills, expending a great amount of energy without any possibility of making headway.

How could she tuck a grown man into bed? Next he'd want her to give him a bath! It was all part of his scheme to send her scampering for home.

If he didn't like his grandfather's plan to polish his rough edges, why didn't he refuse to stay here? He said he didn't want anything to do with the company, so why go through this charade? Why put *her* through it?

She probably surprised him by agreeing to the tuck-in. Most likely he'd only made the offer because he was sure she would nix it.

"Well, two can play his game," she muttered, walking toward the light spilling through the glass door to the bedroom and checking her wristwatch for the hundredth time.

She wasn't even sure which room was Luke's. Mrs. Horning had pointed it out in an offhand way, but there were at least eight bedrooms including hers on the upper floor of the house. Unfortunately, there weren't other guests yet, and the Hornings had an apartment over the garage. She was all alone with a man who was either a genuine beast or a trickster.

Allowing only two minutes to find the right room, she smoothed her wrinkled slacks and reluctantly slipped back into the heavy sweater, buttoning every button as though her life—make that, her virtue— depended on it.

Finding his room turned out to be easy. She'd forgotten the carpeting in the upstairs hallway. Guests could move silently from room to room, but not without leaving footprints in the thick pearly-white plush, newly vacuumed by the housekeeper. His long steps were as easy to follow as tracks in the snow.

She knocked softly, her last hope of reprieve shattered when he immediately called out, "Come in."

After being in her room, elegant with a ruffle-draped four-poster bed and a mirrored dressing table, she was totally surprised by his. It was a shambles.

"Are you trying to get the housekeeper to quit, too?" she asked, taking in the bed stripped to the mattress cover and the haphazard piles of bedding on the floor.

"That mattress is too soft," he complained, impatiently shaking out a king-size yellow sheet and trying to spread it in the area between the foot of the bed and the double door of the closet.

"Why don't you ask for a room with a firmer mattress?"

"I'm settled in here. The floor will do nicely once you get me properly tucked in."

"I can't even get to you. Your stuff's everywhere."

She recognized the battered backpack he'd had in Phoenix, and on top of one of the piles of discarded clothing, was the embarrassingly familiar scrap of what had served as his fountain-dipping attire.

"My laundry," he explained needlessly, pushing aside a heap with his foot.

He was still wearing the hacked-off bush shorts, for which she supposed she should be grateful, but his jacket, tie and sandals were scattered like disaster debris.

She kept her eyes focused on the floor.

"You can start by helping me with this sheet," he said irritably. "It's big enough for a circus tent."

"I'm surprised a hardy adventurer like you needs a sheet."

"Synthetic carpets aren't fit for humans. I'd rather sleep on sand." He scrubbed his knuckles over his rib cage, letting her know the prospect of sleeping on the luxurious plush was enough to make him itch.

"You might try folding the sheet in half," she suggested dryly.

"Take an end," he ordered, flipping the sheet in her direction.

She did, but only because she hoped a little house-keeping help would count as tucking in.

"You're a great little sheet tamer," he said as she spread it with almost no help from him.

He grabbed several thick pillows from a mound on the floor and threw them on his makeshift bed.

"I'll just slip out of these—" he turned his back and unsnapped the top of his shorts "—and you can do the tucking with the other sheet."

"No! Don't you dare!"

"You agreed to—"

"No way."

"Our deal's off, then?"

She bit her lower lip, torn between exasperation and amusement. His performance as an uninhibited wild man was convincing, but she strongly suspected he was doing it to make her back down. What he didn't realize was that she'd been Kim's surrogate mother through her sister's difficult teen years. She could be stubborn when she thought she was right. More than her job was involved now. Darned if she'd let Luke Stanton-Azrat bully or embarrass her into quitting.

"Lie down," she said in what she hoped was a stern, no-nonsense voice.

"Yes, ma'am."

His expression was bland as he hit the floor with one graceful flop and stretched out on his back, cushioning his head on the mound of pillows.

"This is your tuck," she said, making the top sheet from the bed billow over him before it floated down to cover him from head to feet.

"It's not a shroud, love," he said as his head emerged from under it.

"You've been tucked in. Good night."

"Not so fast, Miss Grant. You're not done yet."

He wiggled around under the cloth, then tossed aside his shorts and a scrap of black she tried to avoid seeing.

"Now fold the edges of my sheet like a good nanny. You wouldn't want my toes poking out and getting cold, would you?"

"You're carrying this too far."

"How long will the shopping take?"

"Oh, all right, but freeze—don't move a muscle."

She dropped to her knees and started folding the two sheets together along the edges, making a neat rectangle of his makeshift bed. In spite of her admonition, he stirred enough to make her uncomfortably aware of the contours of his body under the thin covering.

"There," she said when she'd finished, feeling out of breath even though she hadn't exerted herself.

"Nicely done. Now for my story."

"Oh no, I've had enough. I'm done."

His expression was somber, but she was sure he was laughing at her behind those deep blue, unreadable eyes.

"Not till I've had a bedtime story. It isn't a proper tuck-in without one."

"All right, I'll tell you a story," she said through gritted teeth. "Once upon a time there was a prince—"

"A handsome prince?"

"He thought he was hot stuff, but he was really just self-centered and spoiled."

"Self-centered, eh? That sounds harsh."

"I'm telling the story. You're supposed to listen."

"Yes, ma'am."

"The prince thought it was great fun to play tricks on people, especially people who didn't dare fight back."

"He sounds despicable."

She wanted to give him a withering look, but meeting his gaze was too unsettling.

"One day his father, the king—"

"Not his grandfather?"

"This is a fairy tale, not a biography," she said impatiently, boosting herself up to sit on the edge of the bed and put more distance between them. "One day the king got a new slave girl—"

"A smashing beauty?"

"If you like. The prince did some trivial thing to ingratiate himself with the king, so the king gave him the slave girl on one condition."

"Always a condition in these tales," he complained.

"The prince had to be kind to her always."

"That shouldn't have been too hard."

"It wouldn't be for most people, but the prince liked to have everything his own way."

"Something bad is going to happen to this prince, isn't it?" He was grinning now.

"The prince thought he could get away with anything, so he made the slave girl—"

"Do all kinds of nasty things?"

"Stop interrupting! He made her work from dawn to dark with hardly any food, and the king found out."

"The prince is in for it now."

"So the king decided to make the slave girl into a princess and the prince into her slave. That's the end of the story."

"There's no happy ending?"

"For her there was."

"No, not unless she won the heart of the prince."

"It's my story, and the princess sent her new slave to row boats or work in the mines or something."

"What a hard-hearted woman."

"Now you're tucked in. I've kept my part of the deal."

"Have you now?"

He sat up, the sheet falling alarmingly low on his

torso. She started sliding along the edge of the bed to leave without stepping on his sheets, but he caught her foot and pulled off her shoe.

"Luke, don't be silly. Give me my shoe."

"The end of your story needs something—a romantic touch."

"Let go of my foot!"

He ignored her protest and bent his head over her toes, softly pressing his lips against the top of her foot before he slid her shoe back on.

She bolted into the hall, slamming his door behind her.

Her door was the kind that locked by pushing in the handle on the inside, but there was no way to confirm that the mechanism worked. She locked and unlocked the door three times before deciding the flimsy hardware was no defense against Luke if he really wanted to come in. She was being silly. He liked to tease, but he wasn't a threat—to anything but her peace of mind.

Underneath the firmly stretched nylon of her stocking, her foot tingled.

Tomorrow she was going home.

"I'M GOING HOME," Jane said the next morning, passing up the breakfast buffet, but latching on to a cup of coffee as though it were a lifeline.

"Bad idea, love. You've nothing to gain and everything to lose by retreating," Luke said, looking up from his heavily laden plate.

"I'll regain my self-respect," she said, pretending to sip the scalding hot coffee so she wouldn't have to meet his gaze.

"You haven't lost it. I'm the one who's behaved like an ass."

He hadn't intended to apologize. For some odd reason, she seemed to bring out his finer sensibilities.

"Staying is pointless. It's nothing but a big game to you," she insisted.

"Not entirely." He didn't know where to begin or how to explain his curiosity about his grandfather when he didn't understand it himself. "Tell you what. We'll go shopping and—"

"In one store," she dryly reminded him.

"That should be enough," he said blandly. "If I'm not a lamb the whole trip, I'll help you pack."

"You won't dress like the king of the jungle or swing from any chandeliers?"

He deserved her skepticism, but it smarted a bit.

"I promise to be a model shopper. I'm in your hands."

"I have a list of things you're supposed to buy."

"Courtesy of the redoubtable Miss Polk?"

"She's very efficient."

Jane's defense of her boss was pretty lukewarm, Luke decided, but loyalty was an admirable trait, whatever form it took. He found the thought of Janie sticking up for him oddly pleasing—and highly unlikely.

"Where are we going?" he asked, hoping it involved a nice long drive back to Phoenix with Jane beside him.

"There's a very nice shopping center here in Sedona, the Plaza de la Sol. Mr. Cox gets most of his suits made by a tailor there."

"And Miss Polk thinks he'll suit me properly?"

"I've seen your schedule. You need some real

clothes. And Miss Polk is adamant that you get a haircut soon. Next week, for instance, the lieutenant governor will be here and—''

''I capitulate. I'm yours to costume for whatever charade my grandfather has planned.''

''Will you actually wear the new clothes after we pick them out?''

''You're too pretty to be so cynical, love.''

''Stop calling me love! Will you wear them?''

''I will wear whatever you—personally—lay out for me.''

She made a little snorting noise. Apparently his cooperative attitude didn't totally ring true with her.

''We leave in twenty minutes. It's nine thirty-two,'' she said, apparently expecting him to synchronize watches. ''I'll drive.''

Now, that was cruel, he thought. One of the places he really liked to be in control was behind the wheel of a vehicle.

''No need for you to use your car,'' he said cheerfully. ''Granddad loaned me some great wheels.''

She gave him a withering look. ''Be outside in nineteen minutes.''

CONTROLLING THE BEAST in Luke Stanton-Azrat was draining. The fifteen-minute drive felt like a half day's trek over uncharted territory. Her little compact was crowded with Luke scrunched into the passenger seat, and his arm brushed hers every time she had to make a turn. She had to wonder if it was accidental.

Miss Polk's directions were, of course, perfect. Jane not only found the Plaza de la Sol without any trouble, but she had a good idea where to find Javiar's, the exclusive menswear establishment, where the senior partner was waiting for them.

Jane regretted having to rush past all the wonderful shops, among them galleries featuring Southwestern art and Native American crafts, jewelry stores with displays of silver, turquoise, onyx and other gemstones, the Christmas shop, a toy shop catering to the child in everyone, and a fragrant-candle boutique.

But she was eager to hurry through the shady tiled plaza graced by a small fountain with water tinkling through an upraised pitcher held by a concrete cupid. It wasn't hard to imagine Luke stopping to cool his feet in the coin-littered pool surrounding it.

Determined as she was to get him to the tailor's without incident, she couldn't resist stopping at a glassblower's stall. The man was making a whimsical little creature, blowing through a pipe and twisting nimbly to form a fragile swan.

"Isn't that beautiful!" she exclaimed, almost forgetting Luke for a moment. "I wish I could make something like that."

"I'll get it for you," Luke offered.

"No. Thank you, anyway. I just like to watch glassblowers. When I was little, I wanted to work in a museum—be surrounded by beautiful things. Not a very practical career goal."

"Miss Polk definitely wouldn't approve."

"No, she probably wouldn't. Look, there's Javiar's." It was located on the balcony level, sandwiched between a leather goods shop and a store that seemed to sell nothing but beads. She was eager to end their conversation and get this ordeal over with.

"Mr. Cox's assistant made an appointment for

us,'' she said when they joined a reedy young man in a charcoal suit.

''Of course, Miss Grant,'' he said before she could mention her name. ''And Mr. Stanton.''

''Stanton-Azrat,'' Luke said, giving his extra name an odd little inflection that roused Jane's suspicions again.

The proprietor, Mr. Javiar himself, bustled out to greet them. Small and impeccably dressed in a greenish-gray silk-blend suit, he gave the impression he was used to catering to royalty. Luke was definitely going to get the crown-prince treatment.

Three early-bird tourists, forty-plus women overdressed for Arizona but probably at home in East Coast designer showrooms, were pretending to examine hand-loomed neckties while they watched Luke saunter to a small cubicle. He was followed by Mr. Javiar, wielding a cloth tape measure, and his assistant, who carried a clipboard to write down measurements.

Jane hung back, pretending to check out some silk shirts under glass.

''There's one I definitely would like,'' the plumpest of the tourists said with a dignified giggle.

Jane knew darn well they weren't talking about ties.

The dressing room was too crowded to properly shut the curtain. Jane groaned inwardly when she caught a glimpse of Luke's torso, bare to the navel with a jade amulet in the shape of an arrowhead hanging on a leather cord between his spectacular pecs. One of the tourists was openly staring, slackjawed in admiration.

''Waist thirty-three and a quarter,'' Mr. Javiar said

crisply. "Now elevate your left arm, please, Mr. Stanton-Azrat." He made the name sound dignified.

The tape flicked around Luke's hips as though it had a life of its own, and Jane annoyed herself by wondering how much room they allowed for expansion in that particular area. She took a deep breath and decided that, for once, Kim was right. She did need to work on her social life. What she needed was a sweet, sane, reliable man to ward off fantasies about wild ones.

Covering her mouth to conceal a yawn as she imagined dating some nice junior executive, Jane was startled by a female shriek, and horrified when Luke raced past her, a half-sewn shirt clinging to his shoulders like sails on a ship.

He'd bolted!

Okay, he didn't want new clothes, but this was ridiculous. Javiar scurried after him, muttering about expensive silk. His assistant trailed, whipping the tape measure around his hand as though trying to tame it.

Jane stepped out on the balcony just in time to see Luke grab a vine from a plant clinging decoratively to the wrought-iron railing and leap off into space.

"Oh no!"

She raced over to look, expecting to see him lying in a crumpled heap on the red tiles below.

Instead, he was tackling a wiry bald man in a red shirt, and grabbing something from him.

"He got my purse back," one of the tourists cried out, nearly toppling over the railing herself in her excitement.

Jane grabbed the back of her chartreuse-and-black

flowered tunic until the tourist steadied herself, but the woman was too excited to notice.

"Marvelle, he got it back!" She was bouncing with enthusiasm.

Luke hauled the purse snatcher to his feet as the plaza's security guards rushed over to take charge of what turned out to be a shaved-head juvenile, as muscular as Luke but definitely not in his league.

From then on, it was all Luke's show. He was becomingly modest, but still able to milk maximum admiration from the eastern tourists and a crowd of admirers that included the pale-faced tailor's assistant. Mr. Javiar retrieved the shirt remnants, but was hard-pressed to keep a stiff upper lip as his shop began to resemble backstage after a rock concert.

Jane was torn between admiring Luke's heroics and wishing the earth would swallow her up. Against her better judgment, she was impressed by his deed but appalled by the hopelessness of trying to change him to his grandfather's—and Miss Polk's—specifications. He was a man who molded *himself,* and had a great deal of fun in the process.

A security guard took statements. The female tourists fawned over their hero. Half the people in the plaza seemed to be crowded into the shop, all of them babbling with excitement. Luke finally put on his shirt, neglecting to button it.

Jane wanted to congratulate him, but the urge to strangle him was stronger. For a couple of minutes, she thought the brittle-but-well-preserved victim would persuade Luke to accept a reward: lunch, at least.

Jane cornered Mr. Javiar, sympathetic when she

saw his crisp white shirt had wilted, making his neck look scrawny and his chest concave.

"I never expected anything like this," he said in a haughty voice that made her wonder why people who cater to the rich tend to be more pompous than their clients.

"Do you have all the measurements you need?" she asked.

"Yes, but we didn't begin to look at fabrics...." He had a stricken look.

"This is what Mr. Cox wants." She handed him the computer-generated list she'd kept hidden from Luke, hoping to order what Miss Polk called a suitable wardrobe without taking all the choices from him.

"This is—" he finished lip-reading the list "—overwhelming. We need to go over styles, coordinate the accessories, consult on—"

"No, we don't. Mr. Stanton—" she couldn't bring herself to say Azrat without cracking up "—Mr. Stanton needs everything on this list ASAP. If you can't tailor everything yourself to his specifications, we'll settle for off-the-rack. I trust your judgment."

"But, Miss—"

"How long will it take?"

"Six suits, three jackets, formal wear..." He was tallying the list, consternation turning to a highly refined glee. "Say four weeks."

"Four days."

"That's impossible! Even if I employ temporary help—"

"Charge it all to Mr. Rupert's account. He'll be very pleased if his grandson makes a good impression at some very important meetings."

"Four days." His thin lips curled around his words, and he whipped out a gleaming white handkerchief, probably never before used for anything as mundane as wiping away sweat, and dabbed his high forehead. "I'll have to take shortcuts. Mr. Cox never wears anything off a rack. And there will have to be fittings. That's essential for the Javiar look."

"Use a model the same size. His grandson isn't particular." That was the biggest understatement of her life. "Oh, and there's one change. Add Jockey shorts to the list. Two dozen pairs, nice thick hundred percent cotton."

What had she become? She took a downright malicious pleasure in making sure Luke would have practical new underwear—forget those silky black things. She wished she could!

"Sorry the shopping trip was such a fiasco, Janie," Luke said when he had finally torn himself away from the admiring throng. "Tell you what, we'll try again tomorrow."

"No need."

"You're not going home because of the purse snatcher?"

She'd forgotten all about leaving, but she wasn't sure why. Maybe it was the headiness of authority, making such a big—make that, expensive—decision on her own. Miss Polk expected her to guide and suggest. She'd cut to the chase and done the job with precious little help from Luke, other than providing a body for the tailor's measuring tape.

"No, I finalized all the details, that's all," she said, deciding to mention his newly ordered wardrobe later.

"Can I buy you lunch?" He sounded almost penitent.

"Mrs. Horning is expecting us. She's baking scones."

He was quiet all the way to the car. For a moment she thought he was going to open the door for her, then he patted the deep pockets of his khaki shorts, seemingly not finding something.

"Think I forgot something," he said. "Would you mind waiting just a minute?"

"No, but—"

Alone, Jane tried to imagine what he could have left behind.

BACK AT THE MANSION, lunch was so calm and normal, Jane departed the patio table near the pool feeling too sleepy to function.

"I'm going to take a nap," she told Luke.

"Good idea, love."

"Jane," she corrected with little hope of influencing him in any way whatsoever.

Her room was deliciously cool after another meal outdoors in the sweltering heat. Luke had charmed Wilma and seemed determined to spend as little time as possible confined by walls.

She slipped off her shoes and started to turn back the heavy ivory spread when she saw something on the pillow. It was a small black box with gold lettering on the cover.

Almost as puzzled as she was curious, she lifted the cover and took out a small object wrapped in tissue. In a moment she was holding the exquisite handblown glass swan in her palm.

# 5

JANE FELT vaguely guilty for sleeping so late. She was, after all, here to do a job, and a restless night was no excuse to lie in bed until after nine. She showered and dressed in record time, putting on white shorts and a pink shirt without giving it much thought.

She knew how a real nanny must feel: What did her charge get into while she was sleeping? Heading toward the kitchen for her morning coffee, she stopped in Mr. Cox's small but well-equipped office and retrieved a thick sheaf of papers and the latest fax—Luke's homework for the day. He was going to love reading through annual reports, sales figures and labor contracts. What kind of bargain could she strike to win his cooperation? And how was she going to achieve Miss Polk's blunt directive: Get his hair cut.

Right.

Anyway, she liked it long.

She stuck the papers in a manila folder and continued toward the kitchen, feeling a little sorry for herself. She'd gone from being a well-paid errand girl to playing baby-sitter for a wild man. She had as much job satisfaction as a highway worker holding a Slow sign.

"Get those filthy things out of my kitchen!"

Jane walked unnoticed into the room as Mrs. Horning read the riot act to Luke in a strident voice.

"They can't hurt you," Luke said, looking as dumbfounded as Jane felt. "They're just the—"

"I know what they are, and I draw the line at having such things in my kitchen. Get them out!"

"Get what out?" Jane asked timidly, half expecting to see tarantulas scurrying across the floor, her own worst-case scenario.

"I did a bit of hiking in the hills this morning. Came across a dead rattler, run over on a back road," Luke explained. "I have a friend in Botswana who'd give his eyeteeth for rattles like these." He held out his hand to let her inspect his trophies. "Had no idea anyone would object. No poison in the tail."

Mrs. Horning was holding a wooden spoon as though it were a bayonet, but managed to speak more calmly. "Your foreign ways are your business, I'm sure, but I'm terrified of snakes. I want no part of one round me."

"I'm sorry, love. Won't happen again. I'm no hunter anyway. I believe any creature has a right to stay in its natural environment."

He gave Jane a penetrating look she chose to ignore. She wasn't going to leap to his defense; she didn't like his grisly souvenirs any better than the housekeeper did.

"A man has to know where he belongs, too," he said in a somber voice just loud enough for Jane to hear. He went past her and disappeared before she could say anything.

After a few more minutes of sputtering and fretting, Mrs. Horning poured Jane a big mug of coffee fragrant with vanilla and let her escape to the table by the pool. Before sitting down, Jane checked the seats of chairs, the potted plants and the ground around the table. She was a native of Arizona; she knew there were creatures that she'd rather not confront. Leave it to Luke to shatter the imaginary line between ''out there'' and ''in here.''

She was still clutching the folder of papers he was supposed to study. This definitely wasn't the day to worry about haircuts.

As it turned out, she didn't have an opportunity to worry about anything Luke did that day. She was left totally to her own devices, hard-pressed to explain where he was when Miss Polk made her daily call to check on him. At least Jane could report that the wardrobe problem was under control.

When he didn't show up for dinner, she started worrying seriously. His car was there; so were his personal possessions, in considerably better order than the last time she'd seen them. She felt like a sneak, looking in his room to check on him, but like it or not, she was responsible for him. She went to bed, hoping this was just another example of his outrageous behavior.

Of course, there was always the possibility he was out saving another damsel in distress from a petty thief. She didn't like that thought at all. Not at all. Not that she thought he was in danger from common criminals, just from his fawning admirers.

Jane didn't fall asleep that night until she heard the telltale sound of Luke's door being opened and closed. She tried to tell herself it was a relief not to have to tuck him in.

It didn't work.

THE MORNING SUN streaming through the windows did nothing to improve Luke's foul mood. Yesterday's climb hadn't been steep enough, nor the terrain rugged enough, to clear his mind the way he'd hoped. One day of exploring hadn't provided him any more insight into his grandfather or his own reasons for being here.

In fact, it had been dangerous. Not physically, of course—he could handle that kind of challenge. The real peril came from letting Jane inside his head. His gut feeling was that Rupert was using her as bait to keep him in the country permanently. Was the old man doing it without her knowledge or consent? Luke was inclined to believe her innocence was real, not feigned, but that made the attraction he was feeling even more hazardous.

He finished dressing, lacing up his heavy boots for another day of tramping the hills. No doubt Miss Polk had prepared an agenda for him to follow, but she—make that Rupert—wasn't going to pull his strings. If the old man had things to tell him, let him do it in person. Somehow Luke had gotten the impression when they first met that he'd be spending the thirty days getting to know his grandfather, not being groomed by strangers for a job he didn't want.

What was this stay in Sedona, some kind of initiation rite Rupert had engineered to make him worthy of running the company? Luke had no intention of jumping through hoops for anyone. He was tempted to call the whole thing off.

Trouble was, the old devil would probably sack Janie if he left now. Of course, she was a sharp cookie; she could get another job. But would he ever get another chance to understand his grandfather's indifference to him?

This was an odd way to get acquainted with his only living relative, Luke thought sourly, staying in a house with only hired help.

Part of him hoped his would-be nanny would still be sleeping, so he could leave without confronting her. Another increasingly insistent part perked up at the thought of seeing her.

"Janie, love," he said to himself, "you've certainly complicated this little fact-finding mission of mine."

JANE WAS DETERMINED not to allow Luke to sneak out on her again. She set her alarm to ring at the crack of dawn and managed to get downstairs, carrying the manila folder even before Mrs. Horning arrived. If she'd correctly read the tracks on the frequently vacuumed carpeting, Luke hadn't left his room yet.

She started the coffee, made toast from a loaf of whole wheat and smeared it with honey. No skipping breakfast today. She was going to need fuel for maximum energy. No way was Luke-the-Azrat going to evade her or his responsibilities. She'd dressed in denim shorts, running shoes, a short-sleeved blue oxford-cloth shirt and a cotton cap. Wherever he tried to go, she was ready to follow.

"You're up early, Miss Grant."

He managed to enter the kitchen quietly enough to startle her even though she'd been expecting him.

"What are we going to do today?" Her tone said she wasn't in the mood for any of his nonsense.

"Don't know that I've ever had honey like that."

He poked his finger into the carton of spun honey and sucked it with appreciative noises.

"I'll make some toast for you." She moved the honey out of his immediate reach. "It's not nice to stick your fingers into food."

"Three or four eggs lightly over and a rasher of bacon would be smashing," he said, sitting on one of the plank-seat chairs beside a long bleached-wood table.

"I'm not..." She started to say "the cook," but decided it would be a good idea to feed him. She could talk about what he was supposed to do while he was occupied with breakfast. "I'm not very good at fried eggs. I usually break the yolks."

"No problem."

He locked his hands behind his head and stretched out his long, muscular, golden-brown legs. He was wearing battered high-top shoes with heavy socks turned down to cover the top laces. The footgear didn't bode well for a day spent poring over dull business documents.

Actually the breakfast was one of her better culinary efforts: four perfect eggs, the edges brown from the bacon drippings she used to fry them, a plate of crisp, thin-sliced bacon, coffee that tasted almost as good as it smelled and a tall glass of home-squeezed orange juice that Mrs. Horning had left in a pitcher in the fridge.

"Who'd suspect you can cook," Luke said, munching a piece of bacon he'd picked up with his fingers and dipped in yolk.

"Please use a fork when your grandfather's people are here," she begged.

He looked up, grinned and picked up the utensil in question.

"You're absolutely right, Janie. It's boorish of me. And you certainly are one of Rupert's people."

"I didn't mean me." She reached over, snatched a strip of bacon from his plate with her fingers and munched it noisily. Why should she be stuck trying to teach him manners he should have learned from his mother—if his mother had stayed with him. She felt an immense sadness, knowing how she still missed her own mom.

"About today, it's urgent you at least look at these reports before any company execs get here." She pushed the thick folder in his direction.

He flicked open the cover and shuffled through the papers, continuing to eat.

"They look pretty dry. Will there be a quiz?"

"I wouldn't be surprised if Miss Polk stays up all night writing one," she said. "If you flunk, I flunk, too."

"Hardly seems fair." He rested his arms on the table and gazed at her.

"It's business," she said weakly, looking down at her empty coffee cup. "You know, no one is making you go through with this."

"No one can."

"If you really don't intend to go into your grandfather's business, why bother staying here?" Why make *me* stay here, she implied.

"He's my only relative. I thought he might show up at his summer home."

She had no idea where Rupert Cox lived in the Phoenix area. Not gossiping about her boss was another of Miss Polk's admirable but annoying traits.

"I have a few questions for him, and I won't find the answers in this." He pushed the folder away.

"Maybe just an hour—"

"I've taken a fancy to your red rocks. There's a trail I want to follow...."

"I'm going with you, then."

"Isn't that taking your responsibilities a little too seriously?"

"We'll pack a lunch. You have to take a break to eat. You can look through these then." She pushed the pages back toward him.

"You're so set on this, you'll trail along after me in the blazing hot sun?"

"I'll wear a hat, carry plenty of water. Don't think for one minute I can't keep up."

"You can't, not if I've a mind to leave you behind."

"If that's what you want to do, do it. I'm going."

He shrugged, not exactly a show of enthusiasm. Mrs. Horning came in then, still a little cool toward Luke for bringing the snake rattles into her kitchen but willing enough to put together a picnic for them.

"Meet me by the front door in twenty minutes," Luke ordered.

"How do I know you won't leave without me?"

"Janie, you've got to stop being so skeptical. If I say I'll do something, I do it. I give you my word I'll wait for you."

She believed him. Whatever character flaws he had, dishonesty didn't seem to be one of them.

True to his word, he was waiting for her twenty minutes later, an old khaki backpack sitting on the floor by the main entrance.

"Borrowed it from Willard," he said. "If you're

dead set on lugging those papers, you can stick them in my kit. You'll have your work cut out just keeping up without carrying a load.''

"I belonged to the hiking club in high school," she said, miffed by his assumption that she wasn't up to the challenge. "We went on field trips in the mountains and down into the Grand Canyon. You won't have to slow down for me."

His grin was aggravating. If this Neanderthal thought he had a monopoly on stamina, he'd better enjoy eating her dust.

AFTER SEVERAL HOURS of walking, Jane was still keeping up. She had spunk, he had to give her that. He'd pretty well gotten the lay of the land yesterday, and he'd deliberately picked a route that involved the maximum uphill hiking. Part of him wanted her to beg off when the going was rough. Unfortunately, his feelings about her were so mixed, he was enjoying her company immensely. She was witty when she wasn't worried about answering to Miss Polk, energetic enough to keep up with him, and so beautiful with her dark hair tied in a ponytail and bobbing out from under her little hat that he found himself inventing reasons to take her hand or guide her by the arm or fall back and watch the way her calves and buttocks flexed when she climbed.

Worse, he let his imagination run amok, looking for flat rocks and level areas where— Where nothing was going to happen because he was leaving and going back to his natural environment. A man could lose his heart to beauty—in the wilderness of Arizona or in the eyes of a beautiful woman—but Luke couldn't let either be a snare.

HER CALVES WERE TIGHT and achy. Keeping up with Luke was no leisurely stroll, and she hadn't done any serious hiking in a long time. She could handle the discomfort; pride alone would carry her along in spite of it. What was really tough was being with Luke and having him think of her as an adversary, his grandfather's monitor or spy. She found herself wanting to get closer to him. What was under his sometimes breezy, sometimes brash exterior? Why was he staying in Arizona when he didn't seem to have any kind of relationship with his grandfather? Was he really indifferent to the company? Or was she being a fool, reading more into his character than was sensible? Maybe that was it. Her track record with men was abysmal. Relationships without a future were her specialty.

"You okay, love?" He turned and offered his hand to boost her up a steep incline.

"Just fine, thank you."

His fingers were long and hard, gripping her wrist with pressure just short of hurting. She loved strong hands, especially when they were gentle.

"There's a plateau up ahead, a good place for a rest if you're ready for lunch."

"If you're hungry…" She didn't want him to stop because he thought she needed to rest.

"I'm always hungry." He said it in a way that made her doubt he was talking about food.

"All right, we'll stop, then."

The sunbaked, rocky ground was too hot for comfort, but Luke found a small patch of shade and spread a square of checkered cloth. Sitting side by side with his hip wedged against hers, they could hardly avoid touching. They wolfed down sandwiches and shared tea still cool in a thermos.

"Do you mind if I take a power nap, just ten minutes or so?" he asked. "Does wonders for the stamina."

"I thought you'd look through some of these documents while we're resting."

Miss Polk's dreary reports seemed trivial compared to the vivid burnt-orange rock formations and the limitless azure canopy of the sky. She wished her job wasn't on the line, prompting her to act like Miss Polk's clone.

"Give me ten minutes, and I'll give them my full attention," he drawled sleepily.

He stretched out on his back, pulled the visor of his cap over his face, and was either asleep instantly or pretending to be.

She looked at her watch, realizing she had to stay awake to time his nap, or they both might suffer from bad sunburns. The shade barely extended to his shoulders, and his legs already had a ruddy glow under his deep tan.

Minutes passed. Her lids grew heavy. She couldn't imagine anything more pleasant than cushioning her head on his chest and dropping off to sleep.

The heat was fast sapping the last of her energy. Twice her eyes shut, her head bobbing forward to recall her to consciousness. She curled up, using Luke's shoulder as a pillow, not intending to sleep, only rest for a minute.

"WAKE UP, sleepyhead!"

She sat up with a start, realizing what she'd done. "I'm sorry. I got so sleepy."

"No problem. You only dozed a few minutes. Just the thing to recharge your batteries."

She crawled over to the backpack on her hands and knees, drank from a water bottle and extracted the manila folder.

He looked with distaste at the first paper she handed him. "You're not going to hold me to it and make me read this now, are you? You've got to be kidding."

"The sales force will be here Tuesday. Fortunately the lieutenant governor canceled. Wednesday you'll meet the plant manager and—"

"Right."

He handled the document with much the same disdain Mrs. Horning had for snake rattles. Pushing his sunglasses up on the bridge of his nose, he read a line or two.

"This has nothing to do with me."

He tossed the paper back toward her, but it floated downward to the path they'd recently followed.

"I'll get it," she cried out.

She scrambled down, not worrying about the steepness of the incline in her eagerness to retrieve the paper.

Luke called after her, "Jane, let it go! Let me…"

Her left foot started sliding, throwing her onto her back. She couldn't dig her heels into sheer rock, and there was nothing to grasp, no way to stop her downward plunge. She cried out, knowing there was a dropoff below the path, but carried toward it by her own momentum. The sun was blinding, and she couldn't see any way to save herself.

Then she was shadowed by Luke's form leaping past her, and she came to a stop in his arms, braced against him, his body a barrier between her and the dropoff.

"Oh, Luke. Oh!"

"You're okay. Not even a close one. Easy now."

His arms were around her, her cheek pressed against his shoulder, her legs too shaky to support her weight. Her heart was racing, but it only took a moment to realize it wasn't all from fear. She wrapped her arms around Luke's waist, unabashedly clinging, feeling the sturdy columns of his legs hard against hers and his sunbaked cheek caressing her forehead. Sometime soon she was going to start hurting, her back and legs bruised by the fall, but for the moment she was engulfed by pleasurable sensations, loving where she was.

"I have you," he said softly.

He tipped her chin, brushing his lips across her forehead, then stood so still she could feel the beating of his heart.

His lips moved slowly down to the tip of her nose, then pressed against the sensitive bow above her lips. She flattened her hands against his back, wanting him close, wanting…

His kiss was so gentle, she was almost afraid she was imagining it. His lips grazed hers like the tickling of a feather, then he stepped back, effortlessly breaking her hold on his waist and putting an arm's length between them.

"You gave me a scare." He didn't sound light-hearted.

"Me, too. Sorry."

"My fault. I shouldn't have let you bring the damn reports. I had no intention of reading them. Miss Polk can…'' He took a deep breath. ''Maybe we should head back.''

She nodded, but she wasn't at all eager to leave this enchanted place.

# 6

WHAT WAS IT about a kiss that made everything seem upside down and wrong side out?

Jane sat on the edge of the bed, bare toes dug into the plush carpeting, and tried to analyze how she felt about facing Luke over breakfast. Dread? No, not that, even though she was sometimes guilty of letting him intimidate her. Embarrassment? Be serious! She'd been kissed lots of times—vigorous teeth-rattlers, sloppy wet open-mouthers, tongue-to-tongue teasers. Luke's chaste little peck had probably been his way of showing relief that he didn't have to climb down the dropoff to retrieve her lifeless body.

Still, she was tempted to skip breakfast and hole up in her room until he went off somewhere to entertain himself.

Not one of her better ideas! The first contingent of company execs would arrive this evening, and she wasn't—*Luke* wasn't—ready for them. The tailor had promised to deliver at least one presentable outfit by this afternoon, but she still had to get Luke to a barber and coach him on what his grandfather expected.

A simple solution did exist: quit her job. If she couldn't get a well-paying new one right away, she could do temporary work. Thanks to her sister's new job, they could survive without Kim giving up school.

Who was she kidding? This wasn't just about her job anymore. Luke was getting inside her head, wreaking havoc with her emotions. All she had to do was close her eyes to remember the pleasing scent of his sunbaked skin or feel the tickle of his breath on her eyelids.

In less than a month, he'd do what all the desirable men in her life always did: walk away. He'd go back to Africa and life in the wilds, living in construction camps with no room in his life for permanent ties.

She might as well try to do her job and save her career, such as it was, even though she had a better chance of producing a pink-striped giraffe by tonight than a slicked-up, civilized Luke. Groaning loudly, she forced herself to start dressing for breakfast with her boss's beastly grandson.

LUKE BELIEVED in keeping his word, but his promise to stay thirty days was more taxing than he could have imagined. Rupert had baited his hook well. Jane was definitely getting under his skin. If he had any sense at all, he'd be on the next plane out. His plans didn't include falling for a gorgeous American, and he didn't want the complications of getting closer to her.

His grandfather was supposed to arrive in Sedona this evening with some of his minions. Maybe the two of them would have a chance to talk about something besides the company's sports equipment. Or maybe not. Was he making a big mistake, trying to satisfy his curiosity about his mother's father? He'd gotten along fine for years without this family tie.

Maybe he should have left things as they were. He'd waited too long to get acquainted with his grandfather, but before his father's death, it had seemed disloyal to seek out the man who'd vehemently opposed his parents' marriage.

Luke walked naked to the oversize dresser in his room and pulled open the top drawer, amused again by the stacks of pristine white briefs his little keeper had ordered for him. When it came to clothing, his philosophy was simple: less is best. But since Jane was so set on containing his male parts in a sheath of pima cotton, he might as well have some fun obliging her—and in the process annoy her enough to make her forget about his serious slip. Kissing her.

When she'd fallen, his common sense took a header over the cliff. He could still smell the flowery fragrance of her hair and taste the sweetness of her mouth. He should have seduced her then and there and gotten her out of his system, but he'd been afraid—yes, that was the word, afraid. He was already infatuated; he might totally lose it if his fantasies were realized.

He had to put distance between them, and ticking her off seemed the surest way to do it. He slipped into a pair of the new Jockey shorts, pulled on a cutoff tank top that ended above his midriff and padded barefoot down to breakfast.

"Morning, Janie."

She was standing with a cup of coffee, staring out the dining-room window.

"Good morn—"

She froze when she saw him, and he did his best to imitate a fashion model, twirling slowly to give her a good rear view. Women seemed to like a chap's bum, a mystery to him since the fairer sex came equipped with softer, rounder ones of their own.

"Good morning," she said stiffly, averting her eyes but not before she'd seen enough to rattle her. "Mrs. Horning is making muffins. They'll be ready in a bit, just enough time for you to get dressed."

She was playing it cool. He liked that in a woman, but he was counting on his outrageous behavior to make her forget his blunder in kissing her.

"They're a proper fit, don't you think?" He snapped the elastic waistband for emphasis.

"If you say so. I want to thank you for rescuing me. If you hadn't caught me—"

"The least I could do." He sat at the far end of the table, ignoring her suggestion to get dressed and watching intently while she sat on a chair as far from him as possible.

"There was a fax." Her tone was chilly enough to give him goose bumps. "Your grandfather is tied up and won't be able to get here this evening."

"Bloody hell!" The older man was playing games, and Luke was furious at himself for feeling disappointed.

"The others are still coming, so you really have to study the reports today," she said. "And Miss Polk is livid that you haven't gotten a haircut yet."

"None of her concern," Luke muttered, but his anger was focused on his self-important grandfather. What was so bloody important that he didn't have the courtesy to show up?

"I'm sorry you're disappointed," Jane said.

"No skin off my hide," he snapped, standing so abruptly he knocked over the chair.

"He has a lot of responsibilities," Jane said, making a weak stab at defending her employer. "Why don't you give him a call?"

"No way in hell."

He stalked away, feeling ludicrous in the sissy-boy underwear and embarrassed by his dumb stunt. Jane showed real class, considering his boorish behavior, but he couldn't stomach listening to her make excuses for Rupert's behavior. And damned if he'd get his hair cut! What was she planning to do, play Delilah to his Samson? He imagined a naked Jane chasing him with barber's shears, but it wasn't enough to restore his good humor.

He walked past the phone in the living room just as it let out a shrill peal. No way was he going to answer it. There was no one on this continent he wanted to talk to.

Jane caught it on the fourth ring, but by then he was halfway up the spiral steps, intending to dump the whole pile of lily-white undies on Willard and let the caretaker keep or dispose of them. He'd had enough of Miss Jane Grant trying to dress him like a corporation stooge.

He only half heard what she was saying on the phone, but it didn't seem to be a business call. There was concern in her voice, and he only had to hear a few sentences to know something bad had happened.

"Are you telling me everything?" she asked, an edge of panic in her voice. "No—yes—well, call me the minute you're through with the doctor."

"What's wrong?" Luke called down.

"My sister is in the emergency room. I'm more worried about what she didn't tell me than what she did. She fell rock climbing. Says it's only her ankle, but…"

"I'll take you to her. Give me two minutes."

"I can't possibly go to Phoenix now." She started pacing, trying to convince herself, not him. "What timing! I have to see that you get your hair cut, and there's all those reports you're supposed to read before tonight."

"Your sister is more important."

"Kim was adamant about me not coming, but…"

"I'll drive you there. Bring along the reports. I promise not to throw them out the window."

Her lower lip was quivering, and he wanted to offer the kind of comfort that involved taking her in his arms. Instead, he backed away and hoped his smile looked encouraging.

"She promised to call me as soon as she knew anything," Jane said, trying to reassure herself.

"We're going. Do you think we should tell one of the Hornings?"

He sent her to look for the housekeeper while he dashed up to his room, peeled off the constraining briefs and pulled on a pair of faded blue shorts. In less than five minutes he had the Ferrari outside the front entrance waiting for Jane. She didn't forget the stack of papers he was supposed to read.

"I shouldn't go. I shouldn't let you take me."

Impatient because he couldn't let himself take her in his arms and murmur comforting words, he ordered her to buckle up.

"We'll be there in no time. Leave it to me."

He didn't actually burn rubber pulling out of the driveway, but Jane left her stomach behind when they started down the twisting roads.

"You don't have to speed!"

She was a hypocrite, she knew, admonishing him

for driving too fast when she loved the way the sleek sports car held the road. Her pulse raced. Wind whipped hair around her face and made her feel like a kid on a carnival ride. Her fears about Kim were momentarily forgotten as she watched Luke's long, bare legs and powerful arms master the vehicle, taking curves with heart-stopping ease.

They didn't talk much, but he reached over and covered her hand with his.

"I've driven professionally. You don't need to worry about getting there in one piece," he said.

She didn't need reassurances about his driving. He was the only man she'd met who made an automobile seem like an extension of his own prowess. She wanted to blame the insistent tingle running through her on anxiety about Kim, but she couldn't fool herself. Her sensible, sane self knew Luke was driving too fast, but riding beside him in an open car was a terrific turn-on.

By the time they left the hills behind and hit the flat desert north of Phoenix, the Ferrari was chewing up the landscape, flouting Arizona's liberal speed limit. She expected to hear a siren behind them, but the man led a charmed life.

"Why did you quit racing?" she shouted over the wind.

"I wanted something concrete to show for my life, more than prize money and trophies. When I put up a bridge, I expect it to last for centuries."

She was beginning to understand why he'd never be satisfied in a business that made recreational equipment. He'd given her something to think about besides Kim's rock-climbing accident, but once they were close to Mercy Hospital, the frustration of crawling through Phoenix's urban traffic intensified her anxiety for her sister. It would be just like Kim to make light of some horrendous injury. Just the fact that she'd bothered to call meant it had to be serious.

Luke dropped her off at the emergency-room entrance, telling her he'd come to the waiting area after he parked the car.

"My sister is here," Jane told a chubby, pink-faced woman on duty behind the reception desk. "Kim Grant. She fell rock climbing."

"We see a lot of that," the woman said. "Beats me why anyone wants to climb sheer rock to get nowhere. I'd be scared to death of scorpions—snakes, too, but I loathe scorpions. My uncle was bitten once. I remember him telling us kids—"

"Can I see my sister?" Jane interrupted, knowing the friendly Arizona way of doing things might keep her there listening to chitchat for an aeon, not that the woman didn't mean well.

"Go right on back," she said, gesturing. "Someone will point you in the right direction."

She didn't need help locating the partly curtained cubicle where Kim was sitting on an elevated slab, one leg encased in a complicated-looking contrivance. Her sister was telling an animated version of her life history to a lanky young man in hospital garb.

"I don't get much time off," he said after a good laugh, "but I know how to make good use of what I do get. If you're free next Saturday, maybe we could go out."

Jane coughed for attention, but Kim ignored her until she firmed up the date.

"This is my sister, Jane," she said, introducing the resident as Dr. Tom.

"What happened? Are you in pain?" Jane asked.

"Jake said we were going to do an easy climb," Kim explained after her latest conquest sauntered away. "Easy my foot!"

"Why were you climbing so early in the morning? It's not your style."

"Actually I fell yesterday afternoon, but I didn't want to spoil things for the others, so I took some aspirins from the first-aid kit, and Jake wrapped my ankle. We were camping out, but it hurt so much I couldn't sleep all night."

"You should've come to the hospital right after it happened!"

"Well, Tom said it's only a simple fracture, but I have to use crutches for six weeks, and it's going to hurt a lot after the shot wears off. Why can't they give shots in a more dignified place? I told you there was no need to come, but I am glad to see you."

"You told me practically nothing! I've been worried sick. Luke drove like a maniac to get me here."

"He's with you? I'm dying to meet a real wild man. Bring him in."

"Don't worry about Luke. Do you have to stay here?"

"Only until a nurse brings me a prescription for pain pills and some crutches. Good thing I had a lot of practice using them when I hurt my knee."

"Did your friend stick around?"

"Jake left to take the others home. I thought he might come back, but he's not Mr. Reliable. You didn't see him, did you? Big shoulders, no neck. He played football for ASU until he flunked out. No matter. He's history, anyway. I'd rather leave before he gets back. Tell me all about this savage beast you're taming.''

What could Jane say about him? He was an incorrigible, maddening, impossible man, and he made her insides melt.

"I ordered new Jockey shorts for him, and he wore a pair to breakfast," she said impulsively, running one of his stunts past her sister.

"You mean..."

"No pants."

"Wow! Tell me more."

"He doesn't like having me ride herd on him. I don't care for it much myself, but a job is a job."

"Speaking of jobs, I'm just sick I won't be able to work for several weeks. I can get to class all right on crutches, but no way can I wait tables just yet. Jane, I'm so sorry to put all the responsibility back on you."

"Don't worry. We'll get by. I'll get my things and come home."

"No! I'll be perfectly fine alone. You know I'm good on crutches. It would be a disaster if you got fired just to look after me. Anyway, Melinda is going to move in for a while."

Kim was right. Without her sister's income, Jane was trapped. She couldn't leave the company until she had another job lined up, and there was no way to hunt for one while she was stuck in Sedona.

At least Kim's injury didn't sound terribly serious. Luke had been right, though. She'd had to see for herself.

Dr. Tom returned with the prescription, some pill

samples, crutches, a wheelchair and lots of soothing advice.

Silly me, Jane thought, to think Kim needs attention from me. She could go to a wake and leave with a great new boyfriend, unlike her sister, who'd made a career of falling for bad prospects.

Dr. Tom insisted on wheeling Kim out to the waiting room, making a decidedly big fuss over his patient. Jane looked around for Luke, suddenly realizing a Ferrari built for two wouldn't accommodate the three of them.

She spotted Luke sitting in a corner, a pair of gold wire-rimmed glasses perched on his nose, poring over the sheaf of papers she'd pessimistically brought along. She'd never seen him in glasses, and the contrast between his scholarly concentration and sinewy, suntanned muscles rocked her.

"Luke, this is my sister, Kim."

He stood without scattering the papers on his knees, smiled like a movie heartthrob and reached out to shake Kim's hand.

"My pleasure," her sister said, glancing sideways at Jane with a look of unbridled enthusiasm.

Jane gave him a quick account of Kim's condition and directions to their place. He agreed to see something of the city and come for her in two hours so she'd have time to get Kim settled.

"He's the one," Kim said when Luke left.

"He's too old for you."

"Not me, silly. You! Go for it, Jane!"

"It's not that simple. He's going back to Africa."

She knew it would be futile trying to convince Kim she wasn't interested. She couldn't even convince herself.

"You've always wanted to travel."

"He'll be living in construction camps out in the jungle or the bush or whatever."

"Would you rather live in a duplex in Sun City or a tent in paradise? Maybe he could build a tree house. Imagine making love in a leafy bower on an animal-skin rug. It gives me shivers thinking of the possibilities."

"What was in that shot they gave you?" Jane asked dryly.

She called a taxi, and it arrived to take them home. Kim wouldn't stop talking about Luke, asking questions that made Jane squirm. When her sister asked if Luke had kissed her yet, Jane almost wished Kim had fractured her jaw instead of her ankle.

Back at the apartment Jane settled Kim on the thrift-store couch covered by a red, white and yellow flowered chintz slipcover they'd made together. She changed sheets on both beds, washed some dishes and cleared away debris that might trip her sister as she hopped through the place on crutches.

"There's enough food so you won't starve," she told her sister. "I'll leave some cash so Melinda can go to the store if you need anything."

"Thanks, but you're the one who's starving." Kim's voice sounded slurred from the painkiller she'd taken, but she was still focused on her favorite topic: Jane's love live—or lack thereof.

"Don't say it," Jane warned.

"Starving for love. Really, Jane, this one is a winner. All that golden hair, bulging muscles and coppery skin. You'd never get cold at night cuddled up with him."

"This is Arizona. I only get cold when you set the air-conditioning too low."

"You've got to get out of that born-again virgins club. If I didn't know about Bryan, I'd think you'd never—"

"Don't think! And stop giving me a sales pitch about Luke Stanton-Azrat. He's made it clear his life-style isn't compatible with a wife and family. All I want from him is a tiny bit of cooperation—enough to stop his grandfather from firing me. When I leave the Cox Corporation, I want to hand my resignation to Miss Polk."

"Has she been to Sedona?"

"No, but her spirit haunts the place via fax."

Jane checked her watch, wishing she had her own car. Why had she let Luke rush to the rescue? She didn't need or want a big strong man to solve her problems.

When he did arrive, forty-seven minutes late, Kim was so groggy from painkillers, she was hard-pressed to tell him Jane's whole life history in the half hour he stayed drinking herbal tea, prepared by Jane at her sister's insistence.

"Jane is quite a woman," Luke said, grinning and getting into the tell-all-about-Jane spirit. "She did a capital job fixing me up with a corporate wardrobe. You should see the stack of—"

"Luke," Jane said, "we really have to get back. People are coming just to meet you."

"Sorry, love," he said to Kim, leaning over and kissing her forehead. "When your sister's right, she's right. Can't have a circus without the clown."

Kim giggled. She thought everything Luke said was hilarious.

"Take care now," he said warmly. "If you need anything, just give us a call. We can be here in two shakes of a lion's tail. Make that a monkey's. Papa lion is the laziest creature on earth. Does nothing but eat, sleep and—"

"Luke, we have to leave!" Jane interrupted.

"...keep the females happy."

"Should I call you Daddy Lion?" Kim teased, keeping her lids propped open by never taking her eyes off Luke.

"When will Melinda be here?" Jane asked, standing by the door but still reluctant to leave her sister alone.

"I've told you twice." Sometimes Kim could be a brat. "She gets off work at five."

"Meanwhile, you get some rest," Luke said, patting her shoulder.

Jane said goodbye and walked out to the parking area just in time to snatch up several pages of confidential reports as they blew out of the Ferrari. Luke had tossed the pile on the passenger seat without returning the sheets to their large manila folder. The pile was considerably reduced from what she'd given him. Insider information was probably floating all over Phoenix, and she had a pretty good idea who would be blamed if any got into the wrong hands.

"You're littering with sensitive company documents," she said as soon as he got close to the car. "Your grandfather will—"

He walked up to her, put both hands on her shoulders and loudly smacked his lips against hers. As a kiss, it was close to a nine; as a way of shutting her up, it was playing dirty.

"Don't do that!"

"I already have. Give up, Janie. I read the blasted things. There's nothing in them that interests me. I apologize for littering, but not for thinking they're garbage."

He picked up the pile, jogged over to the side of the building where the Dumpster was partially concealed by a brick wall, and deposited the lot in the trash.

She was afraid to object. His new method of silencing her was too hard on basic body chemistry. Her hormones were doing a rumba south of her navel.

The last thing she needed was to be scooped up by the golden gorilla and dumped into the passenger seat, but that was exactly what happened.

"You have no right to—"

"Buckle up, love. We've got a date with some clock punchers."

"Don't drive so fast this time. We'll get there in time."

"Glad to hear it. Afraid I was late getting to your place. I wanted to see the botanical gardens, and there was more there than I expected. Never saw so many cactus—cacti—and quite a crop of Homo sapiens, too. Most endangered species on the planet, but they haven't realized it yet."

"I'll put it on tomorrow's list of worries."

"Your sister will be fine. Plucky kid. A shame she'll be off work. Means you're pretty much stuck for the duration."

"The duration?"

"Of my visit to your fair land. I am leaving when I've done my time."

She'd be glad to see him go—or would she?

He honked at a motorist who tried to switch lanes by cutting him off. Jane always gave pickup trucks with gun racks the right-of-way, but Luke streaked ahead, letting them eat his dust, figuratively speaking.

The freeway out of town was clogged with rush-hour traffic, but Luke always found an opening, leading the pack without being an exhibitionist or endangering anyone.

The revolution of the wheels hummed through her, vibrating from the soles of her feet. She wanted to put her hand on Luke's thigh and feel the surge of the engine pulsing through him.

Wanted to, but didn't.

Flings weren't her style. Besides, he was strictly a temp on the mating scene, no matter how nice it would feel to rub her leg against his golden-haired calf or let her fingers wander over his lean, sun-browned midsection and chest. He had the kind of torso that had made Victorian matrons flock to museums to gape at chiseled marble statues.

She was hot and thirsty. Closing her eyes, she imagined sparkling water, an azure pool with a classical nude statue, face raised to the spray. The statue moved and became Luke, poetry in flesh, fully aroused and waiting for someone, for her....

Something nudged her arm.

"Sorry to wake you, Janie, but the engine is overheating. Probably happened when we were stuck in traffic without moving for twenty minutes. I need to get some water for the radiator."

"Oh, I didn't know." She was glad her face was red and hot from the late-afternoon sun so Luke couldn't tell she was blushing. He'd interrupted her dream at a crucial moment; she could still feel the statue-come-to-life slipping between her bare thighs and—

"This is as far as we go until it cools," he said, sounding pretty cheerful for a guy whose car was acting up on a desert highway. "Good luck for us, though. If that sign is right, we're only half a mile from a petrol station."

She looked up at a sand-scoured sign set well back from the road on private land: Jackrabbit Acres.

"That's not a good place, Luke. Not a good place at all."

"We're fresh out of choices. Anyway, how bad can it be?"

"Think bikers' hangout, chains, switchblades, blood."

"Sounds colorful. Come on. It's not the Sahara, but I don't want to leave you out here in this heat."

"August in the desert is no place for a picnic," she said, reluctantly getting out to trudge along the highway beside him.

Luke took her hand, staying on the traffic side.

People didn't perspire in the Arizona desert; they dehydrated. Jane's mouth was cottony, and her lips felt rough from dryness. Before they'd gone half the distance, she felt light-headed and slightly disoriented, as though this was part of her dream.

"You all right, Janie?" Luke stopped and touched her cheek with the backs of his fingers. "Bloody fool! Me, not you. I thought being a native, you were immune to the heat."

"I live in air-conditioned splendor," she said, giggling for no reason.

"Here's just the thing."

He pulled a large red bandanna from the back pocket of his shorts and folded it to make a head covering for her.

''Hang on. We'll get some fluid into you pronto.''

Jackrabbit Acres had modernized the gas pumps, but nothing else. The combination saloon, general store and all-round hangout was a long wooden building bleached silver by fifty years or more of blowing sand. A porch with dusty board railings ran the length of the place. A weathered wooden bench offered some blessed shade, but a trio of bikers had pretty much taken it over, sprawled out guzzling beer and cussing the heat, warm brews and each other. One with shaggy, greasy blond hair and a filthy black sweatband seemed to be the leader. All three wore creased black leather pants and high boots. One was wearing a denim jacket, but the other two wore vests on bare upper torsos covered by crude tattoos and sweaty, matted hair.

Jane tugged on Luke's hand, hoping he'd skirt around them and follow a battered sign that said Deliveries in the Rear. Instead, he barged right up to the ugliest and biggest of the trio.

''A hog just like that passed me ten, fifteen minutes ago,'' Luke said, pointing at one of the motorcycles parked a few yards away. ''Great machine. I was doing ninety, and the bugger made me eat dust.''

The ferret-faced biker was leering at Jane with bleary, red-rimmed eyes. She was too light-headed to do anything but cower by Luke's side and wish the earth would swallow her up.

Luke talked the talk. Even Mr. Rodent-Face

stopped ogling her and expressed an opinion about camshafts and pipes.

"Be a good race if you could catch him," Luke suggested. "I don't know how, though. Same machine, twenty-minute start."

The dirty blonde swore and spat, and the three bikers tossed their cans aside, mounted their bikes and took off in a storm of dust and exhaust.

"Do you think they'll catch him?" she asked.

"Not likely." Luke grinned at her.

"You made that up."

"Too hot to take on all three of them," he drawled lazily. "Sit here. I'll get something to cool us off."

She leaned her head back against the splintery board wall, closed her eyes and wondered where she'd get the energy to walk back to the car. Luke could pick her up here, but she didn't want to deal with any more bikers on her own. She definitely didn't know the lingo.

"The owner's filling a gallon jug for the car," Luke told her when he came back. "These sodas aren't too cold, but we can cool down another way."

She took a can of cola from him and looked skeptically at the battered pie tin he was carrying.

"Ice cubes. The old boy parted with them for a price. Lean back and close your eyes."

"Why?" She took a big swallow of cola and did as he asked when he didn't offer an explanation.

"Let yourself relax," he said softly. "Just trust me."

Did she have a choice?

He lifted her right hand and cupped it in his palm, then slid a cube over her sensitive inner wrist. After the initial icy shock, her skin numbed and absorbed the wonderful, cooling dampness.

"It really works," she said with drowsy amazement.

"No talking."

He slid another cube over her inner elbow, making her shiver with pleasure, then did the same to her other wrist and arm.

"Mmm."

The cubes were slippery now, and he ran one over her forehead and cheeks, then down to the V-shaped neckline of her lemon-yellow cotton knit top.

"I'm cool now, really cool," she gasped, guessing what he had in mind next.

The cube slid down to the hollow between her breasts, small and slippery but still cold enough to make her cringe.

"Enough," she begged, but he was already sliding a fresh ice cube over the back of her knee.

She had too much imagination. She couldn't help wondering how an icy trail up her thigh and over her pelvis would feel, his cold fingers creating magic on overheated flesh.

"Oh!" Her moan came from way down deep and embarrassed her enough to break the spell. "I'm as cool now as I care to be."

She gulped more soda to cover her agitation.

"I'm not."

"You expect me to—"

"Turnabout is fair play."

"But it's your game."

"You're cool and comfortable now."

"Oh, all right." She didn't try to sound gracious.

"Wherever you like," he said, pushing the pan of

rapidly melting ice cubes in her direction, stretching
out his legs and resting his head against the wall.

She picked up a slippery cube and lifted his hand.
His fingers curled when she stroked his wrist with
the fragment of ice, and she knew why he groaned
with satisfaction.

She looked over her shoulder, relieved there were
no other customers at the moment, and fished another
cube from the water forming on the bottom of the
pan. She was enjoying this more than she wanted to
admit.

The contrast between the ice and the heat of his
forehead gave her odd little shivers.

"There," she said when she finished sliding a
piece over his throat. "You must be cooler now."

"Not quite," he whispered in a husky, spine-
tingling voice. "There's still a lot of me to cool
down."

His shorts had a single button above the suspi-
ciously bulging zipper, she noticed, as a noisy pickup
truck pulled off the highway, heading down the
bumpy gravel road to Jackrabbit Acres. She scooped
up the slippery remains of the cubes in one palm,
quickly undid the button that held the waistband taut
against his torso and pushed wet ice pieces under the
zipper.

He jumped up, slivers of ice falling to the ground
from the legs of his shorts.

She was too embarrassed to look at him. Her trick
had backfired badly. He'd shed his nice new briefs.
She'd touched all man instead.

She started tramping back to the car without him,
fuming about his uncivilized ways. What kind of
man went around not wearing underwear?

When he caught up, carrying the plastic milk jug of water, she was sitting in the car, eyes closed, pretending to sleep so she wouldn't have to look at him or talk to him.

''I owe you one,'' he said softly after he closed the hood and sat beside her to start the engine.

She had no doubt he'd pay her back.

# 7

SHE WAS FEIGNING sleep, and it suited him to let her.
He was still amused—and thankful—for her prank.
It had brought him to his senses, but she didn't need
to know that. Far from cooling him down, it had had
the opposite effect. He'd wanted to follow the trick-
les of melted ice on her skin with his tongue. He'd
ached to retrieve the slivers of ice between her
breasts.

He'd even been tempted to see if Jackrabbit Acres
had rooms to rent by the hour. Fortunately, the cascade of wet ice had brought him to his senses. She
wasn't a one-night-stand kind of woman; he couldn't
get intimate without hurting her, and he liked her too
much to allow that to happen. Intellectually she knew
he would be leaving, but women got funny ideas in
the afterglow of sex.

What would he do with Jane in the camps? True,
a few engineers tried bringing their wives with them,
but it never worked out. His own parents were proof
of that. Even the spunky ones who could handle the
primitive living conditions—and his mother hadn't
been one of them—succumbed to boredom. Bridge
builders worked from dawn to dark with only a short
break to escape the noon heat. There was no social
life for a woman, no amenities and little contact with
family, friends or the world at large.

*It's not for you, Janie,* he thought, feeling an odd tightening in his midsection when he glanced over and saw her long, spiky lashes flicker and the moist pink tip of her tongue touch her lower lip.

"Awake, are you?" He couldn't resist any longer. He enjoyed talking to her almost as much as he'd liked planting a hard kiss on her parted lips.

"We should get there with a half hour to spare to get cleaned up," she said.

"You look fine the way you are, and I'm not about to prepare for a spit-and-polish inspection by a bunch of suits."

He even liked the way she pouted, her lips more kissable when they were slightly puckered. He wasn't very happy about his wild-man stunts, though. Everything he'd done to make himself look bad had put distance between them, but he wasn't comfortable knowing she didn't entirely trust him.

*You don't have a place for her in your life, so it doesn't matter,* he told himself without conviction.

He spotted trouble as soon as he pulled into the driveway in front of his grandfather's summer home: two Cadillacs, a Mercedes and a limo with a uniformed driver shining the windows. The company big guns had arrived early, probably another of Rupert's ploys to wear him down.

"Oh, dear," Jane said with real distress.

He gave her hand a reassuring pat, then swung himself out of the Ferarri without opening the door. His philosophy on taking his licks was to get it over with.

"Why don't you go around to the kitchen door?" he suggested. "No need for both of us to get dressed down."

"No, you were nice to drive me to Phoenix. It's my fault we weren't here when they arrived."

Arguing with her was like punching a wall of foam rubber: no pain and no gain. At least his grandfather wouldn't be here to give her a hard time. He did wonder, though, who was high enough in the company to rate a limo.

Luke led the way into the house, still wishing Jane would make herself scarce. He heard the tinkle of ice in glasses and the monotonous buzz of conversation before he saw the group standing around in the main room. Three men in dark suits and conservative neckties were trying to kill time, probably saying the same old things they always said to each other. Then he saw the fourth visitor, his silver-haired grandfather, sitting in a big leather armchair like a king holding court.

"Luke, where the devil have you been?" Rupert roared. "Horning said you had to chase down to Phoenix. Some kind of accident."

"That's my fault, Mr. Cox," Janie said, gamely stepping forward. "My sister fell rock climbing, and Luke drove me down to the hospital."

"We net two mil a year on gear for fool kids climbing rocks. Could do a lot more if—"

"Her sister will be all right," Luke interrupted, annoyed by his grandfather's obsession with business.

"Glad to hear it," he said automatically. "But you look like roadkill. Where're all the new duds I had Miss Grant buy for you? You look like you just got off a banana boat."

"Granddad, I thought you weren't going to come."

"Changed my mind," Rupert said brusquely.

The execs had managed to inch their way to a far corner, out of their boss's sight but still able to soak up every word for later analysis.

"You study all those papers I had Polk send?" the older man went on.

"Yes, sir. I'll be glad to sit down and discuss them after I've had a shower."

Rupert looked at a Swiss wristwatch with more dials than the cockpit of a 747 and grunted disapprovingly. "I'd like to hear what you think now."

Forgotten by the men, Jane was slowly backing away but hesitated when Luke plopped his dusty, sweaty, but still sexy body into a white chair. She knew he'd read at least some of the papers, but if her pupil flunked Mr. Cox's examination, she was the one at fault.

"What you need, sir," Luke said, "is to drop your least profitable lines and maximize promotional efforts where they can do the company the most good."

Luke had everyone's attention. Mr. Cox picked yes-men as his underlings. No one, with the possible exception of Miss Polk, ever made suggestions that weren't substantiated by several inches of computer printouts.

"As I see it," Luke went on, "the 'bigger-is-better' acquisitions of the eighties left you strapped for top-notch talent, so you made your management structure top-heavy."

The minions, top men in accounting, production and promotion, were closing in, sensing a threat to their domains. Jane was too dazzled by Luke's performance to enjoy their throat-clearing mumbles.

Luke was making intelligent comments, pinning down problems like a corporate raider about to pounce. For a man who didn't want anything to do with his grandfather's sporting goods empire, he was spouting facts and figures like an Ivy League MBA.

Luke glanced at Jane, as dusty as he was with her nose and knees sunburned and her hair windblown under the bandanna he'd tied on her head. He was out of his mind, making his grandfather think he cared a whit about desk-jockey issues. He was only doing it to blow smoke in Rupert's face and keep him from coming down hard on Janie. The older man had looked ready to fire her on the spot when they showed up looking like desert rats.

Luke quoted enough facts from the reports he'd filed in the Dumpster to make his grandfather believe he'd spent days poring over them, but he wished Jane would get her tail upstairs before Rupert noticed her again. The old man wasn't going to be impressed by a stack of pima cotton underpants, while Luke continued to wear the wardrobe he'd brought from Africa wadded up in a knapsack, which he fully intended to do.

"How would you cut down on top-heavy management?" his grandfather asked shrewdly. "Attrition?"

"Too slow. If you wait for the forty- and fifty-somethings to retire early, you won't have any vigorous young execs trained to breathe life into the company."

"Strong stand." Rupert looked impressed but unconvinced.

Damn! All he was doing was making his grandfather more determined than ever to involve him in the company. It was bad enough he'd agreed to stay six weeks. Now Rupert would pull out all the stops to teach him the Cox way of managing a company Luke never intended to head.

Luke kept talking, but his mind was on Jane. He must be crazy, playing his grandfather's game just to save her job. She wasn't his worry. He was complicating his life even though he had every intention of leaving the States without her. He wished he could stop thinking about her, but he was burning to sample that sweet, seductive mouth again and hold her in his arms with nothing between them. It wasn't enough just imagining the contours of her breasts; he needed to hold them in his hands and taste them with his mouth.

He wanted her; she wanted him, or would if he really tried to seduce her. Why couldn't things between a man and a woman be simple and satisfying?

JANE WAS GRATEFUL to Luke for performing so well for Mr. Cox, but surprised by his astute comments. Was he wavering in his rejection of his grandfather's offer to take over as CEO? She found that hard to believe. He'd never be happy cooped up in an office dealing with petty office politics, not to mention wearing business suits and starched collars.

She retreated to her room, grateful for a chance to shower and change into a sleeveless black crepe dress, simple but dressy enough for dinner with the sharp-dressed company men. Or did she dare skip the meal? She was only hired help, but unfortunately, the boss wanted her there.

She dawdled in her room, dreading the time when she had to go downstairs. What was Luke up to? He was an enigma, sending out signals she couldn't mistake even though he'd made it plain that anything between them was impossible. So why did it hurt knowing he'd soon walk out of her life forever?

She thought of inventing a headache as an excuse to miss the meal, but didn't. Much as she dreaded sitting down to dinner with Mr. Cox, Jane was too curious about Luke to beg off. She descended the spiral stairs, wary of calling attention to herself even though Luke had acquitted himself well in her opinion. He'd thrown down a gauntlet for the execs gathered there, challenging his grandfather to cut dead wood and modernize his operation.

The CEO didn't like changes unless he thought of them.

A nervous shiver tickled her spine as she walked into the room where the men were gathered.

Something was wrong. Luke and his grandfather were alone at the far end, walking a yard apart toward the front entrance.

Cox wasn't staying for dinner.

"Miss Grant." He summoned her with a bullhorn roar. "Didn't Miss Polk give you the name of my barber in Sedona?"

"Yes, sir, she did."

Then, turning to Luke, "See that you get your hair cut before Saturday," he ordered Luke. "It'll be a little get-together outside Sedona for some of my friends to meet you. People you need to know. I'll expect you to be there, too," he said, nodding at Jane.

Luke didn't respond, but Jane could see the tension in his squared shoulders and clenched hands.

His mouth was set in a tight line as he watched his grandfather walk over to the limo and get in.

If Luke wanted Rupert to stay, why didn't he ask him? Jane tried to convince herself that their relationship was none of her business, but she couldn't help wondering what had motivated Luke to come to the States in the first place. Why was he staying when there didn't seem to be any warmth between the two men? She still believed he wasn't interested in the company or his grandfather's fortune.

What was keeping him here?

He muttered something that made her ears burn and gave her a cold glance.

"Dinner should be ready," she said, falling back on an inane comment because she didn't know how to deal with the pain in Luke's eyes.

"Enjoy," he said rudely. "I'm not dressed for polite society."

He stalked out the front door, leaving her to face the hostile curiosity of the Cox execs.

"Will you be joining us—it's Miss Grant, isn't it?" the head of accounting asked.

Was she supposed to play hostess? Obviously these men thought so. They were practically standing in formation waiting for her to give the signal for the meal to begin. She looked at the open doorway and made a rash decision.

"Please go ahead without me, gentlemen. I won't be joining you for dinner."

She rushed out the door in pursuit of Luke. The Ferrari was still there, so he must have decided to walk off his anger or frustration or disappointment— whatever it was that simmered between him and his grandfather.

Following the neatly manicured footpath that wound around the house, she hurried to check out the rear patios, hoping Luke hadn't taken to the road. She wouldn't get far in her heels tracking him in the hills.

She found him in the pool.

Checking for discarded clothing before she got too close, she saw the contents of his pocket and his watch on a small metal table beside a lounge chair. His tank top was crumpled on the plastic cushion, but his shorts were nowhere in sight, making her hope he was swimming in them. She approached the pool with a somewhat easier mind, standing on the edge until he completed a lap and grabbed on to the rim inches from her feet.

"I'm sorry your grandfather didn't stay," she said.

"If you want to talk to me, come on in."

"I'm not in the habit of swimming in a dress," she said stiffly, trying to establish distance between them.

His hair was clinging to his head the way it had that morning under the company fountain. He had terrific bone structure, with high cheekbones and an aggressive jawline that went beyond handsome.

"Live recklessly for a change, if Rupert and his flunkies don't have you totally cowed. Take off your dress and dive in."

"How do you know I can swim?"

"You don't need to. I'll hold you up." His smile was infuriating.

"I'm supposed to trust you not to let me go under?"

A few minutes ago he'd looked miserably unhappy. Now he might as well beat his chest like a male gorilla, he was sending that kind of message.

Of course, he didn't think she'd do it. He was angry at his grandfather, and his release was to bait her.

She ambled over to the table, casually removed her watch and little gold earrings, then stepped out of her heels, worn without hose because her knees smarted from sunburn. With one quick zip, she let the dress fall to her ankles and stepped out of it.

Ignoring his low whistle, she stepped up to the edge of the pool in her ivory lace bra and panties and dived in. She did three fast laps before acknowledging him swimming beside her, practically matching her stroke for stroke.

"Where did you learn to swim like this, love?" he asked, trapping her between his arms when she paused at one end of the pool.

"Not in a jungle pond. My sister and I learned at the Y."

"You learned well."

He looked good wet—no, that was an understatement. He looked fantastic, drops of water beading on sun-bronzed skin, his hair streaming water over powerful shoulders and trickling down the silky hairs plastered on his chest. His nipples made her uncomfortable; she tried not to look at the hard, masculine points.

"You were angry when your grandfather left." She was putting him off by deliberately playing the heavy, calling him to account for his behavior.

"Let it be, Jane."

"If you're not happy with him, why not just leave?"

"It's not that simple."

He kicked away, swimming to the other end of the pool. She didn't follow; she'd seen the way he looked down at her breasts, damply encased in almost transparent fabric, and was sure he'd come back to her. Was she in the pool to better understand him or to have him hold her in his arms? She wasn't sure.

"I gave my word to stay in Sedona for thirty days. You know that," he said flatly, breaking water beside her, then immediately resuming his lap to the other end.

Well, she'd certainly been told. The only reason to stay in the pool was to watch him slice through the water with heart-stopping ease. And to avoid climbing out in her skimpy panties.

He did three more laps before he stopped beside her again.

"I can't thank you enough for driving me to the hospital. Kim really scared me when she called. She's all I have, and family is really important to me."

"Not to me."

"Luke, you don't mean that. You came all this way to get to know your grandfather."

"I've satisfied my curiosity about Rupert Cox. That's all it was. Curiosity."

"I don't think you have."

"Think whatever you like. I'm heading back when my time is up. Nothing can keep me here. I hope you understand that, Jane."

He wasn't just talking about his grandfather. He was warning her not to expect anything from him, not to feel anything for him.

He was too late.

"Are you up to a race?" he said. "My five laps to your three. Loser pays a penalty." His voice was light and teasing again.

"What penalty?"

"Winner's choice."

"I want you to get a haircut." She didn't, but she wasn't exactly in Rupert's good graces.

"Agreed—if you win."

"What do you want?"

"I'll think of something."

"Luke!"

"If you're afraid…"

"Of you? I don't think so. On your mark, get set—"

"Go."

To his credit, he gave her a second's head start, then swept past her, hardly rippling the water.

She wanted to win, needed to win, was counting on his extra laps to make it possible.

When he won by half a lap, she knew he'd been toying with her. He moved through the water like an Olympic champion, and a two-lap advantage wasn't enough.

"You knew you'd win." She was breathless and mad at herself for accepting a sucker bet.

"No, you made a contest of it."

She slapped the water, throwing spray on his face, but he only laughed it off, drawing her into the circle of his arms and treading water for both of them.

"Do you want to know what your penalty is?"

"I can hardly wait," she said dryly.

"What I'd really like is to have you spend the night with me."

"No!"

''Let me finish. That's not it. I'll settle for a nice kiss.''

''Oh, all right.'' She'd secretly hoped the penalty would be pleasant to pay.

He reached down and cupped her skimpily clad bottom, drawing her so close his knee slid between her thighs.

''Just a kiss, you said.''

She'd never been more ready and willing, but she hated herself for wanting a man who felt nothing but physical attraction for her. If he had any real feelings for her, they were so deeply buried they might never surface. She knew the deal: he was leaving. Alone. He hadn't left any room for negotiating.

''A kiss at a time and place of my choosing,'' he said firmly.

''This isn't it?''

She felt weak with disappointment, or maybe the swimming competition had drained all her energy.

''You'll know when the time comes,'' he promised.

# 8

HAIR, hair, hair! Jane wanted to scream. What was this obsession with cutting Luke's hair? He wasn't a marine recruit!

She crumpled the latest fax from Miss Polk and filed it in the wastebasket, suspecting her immediate supervisor was the one insisting on a makeover before Luke made his first official public appearance. If Rupert really was eager to have his grandson join the company, he should have enough sense not to make an issue over hair. Luke wasn't a servile peon like everyone else—herself included unfortunately.

Admittedly, barbers would starve if they waited for Luke's business, but Jane loved the wild-man look, the heavy sandy mane lightened by the sun and brushing his wide shoulders. It made him look unrestrained and untamed—and very, very sexy.

She hated this job. Just being in the same room with Luke made her edgy. Maybe a good clip job would take away some of his appeal, make him look more ordinary. She hadn't urged him to humor his grandfather in the past several days, but the party was tomorrow. She had nothing to lose by suggesting it—if she could find him. He'd gone off by car or on foot every morning since his grandfather's visit, once not even returning for dinner.

Whatever her boss expected her to accomplish

here, she was actually getting paid for lounging by the pool. Anyone who thought she had a soft job should try killing time as a vocation. It was considerably harder than real work.

She was in luck today; she caught up with Luke just as he was going out to his car.

"Are you in a hurry to go somewhere?" she asked, tagging along after him.

"Thought I'd go to the Grand Canyon and ride a mule to the bottom while I'm still in the area. Care to come along?"

"Done that, thanks. I started the trip feeling sorry for the mule and ended feeling sorry for me. The sun will be broiling hot, and mobs of tourists will have the same idea. Spring and fall are better times to go."

"Afraid I won't be here then. Maybe you know a better way to pass the time?"

Today he sounded more like the wild man she'd chased out of the fountain. The brooding, solitary Luke of the last few days was a little scary.

"I know a great little place in town—comfy chairs, soft music, personal attention...."

"Are you trying to con me, love?"

She shrugged her shoulders. "Thought it was worth a try. You're not going to a barbershop, are you?"

"Not unless you throw me over your shoulder and carry me there."

"Very funny. You're making my job awfully difficult, and Kim is counting on me."

"How is little sis?"

"Doing pretty well. All she talked about on the phone last night was her personal physician. Dr. Tom checks on her constantly. Well, have a nice day."

"Wait a sec, Janie. My itinerary isn't written in concrete. Do you have a better idea?"

"No, I'm not much of a tour guide."

"Keep me company, and I'll agree to a bush cut."

"Do you mean brush cut?" She was mildly horrified.

"No, a cut the way we do it in the bush. I sit still for five minutes, and you click the shears around my head."

"*Me* trim *you?* Be serious! I can't cut hair."

"I'm sure you can't, at least not like a professional, but a chimpanzee can be trained to use scissors."

"Thank you for the comparison." She wasn't as put off by his suggestion as she wanted him to think.

"Never saw a chimp with legs like yours. Why not give it a try?"

Why not indeed? She had to hang on to this job while Kim's ankle healed. If Luke trusted her close to him with a sharp instrument, why not give it a try?

He went upstairs to shampoo, while she borrowed scissors, a broom, dustpan and a tablecloth to drape around his shoulders from Mrs. Horning. When he was seated on the patio overlooking the pool, she secured the cloth with a wicked-looking safety pin.

"You and Sis have cut each other's hair, I imagine," he said, squirming a little while she made a center part with his comb.

"She wouldn't let me touch her crowning glory for a round-trip to Hawaii," Jane teased, making a tiny tentative snip.

"Ouch!"

"That didn't hurt," she said, wondering how to proceed.

The stylist who cut her hair sectioned it and used clips. She tried dividing it that way with her fingers, enjoying the closeness to Luke.

It made sense to her to start at the back and work around to the sides, but how much should she take off?

"Just a light trim," he warned ominously.

"Two inches?"

He shook his head, not doing anything for her concentration.

"At least one inch," she said firmly, doubting her employer would notice such a minor difference. But hair was part of a person's self-image; only the owner should decide how to wear it.

"It will take all day if you cut one piece at a time," he commented. "Or maybe you like being close to me?"

"No such thing!" she protested a little too vehemently.

She edged along first one side, then the other. His hair was nearly dry, warm and silky to the touch, but the ends crackled with life. The part she enjoyed most was checking for errant strands, letting his locks caress the sensitive skin between her fingers.

Now all she had to do was make sure the two sides were even. She stepped between his widely spread legs, combing to check for lopsidedness. His thighs felt hot against her bare legs, and she wished she'd vetoed his idea of doing this outside. She was close enough to get dizzy on the faintly herbal scent of shampoo mingled sensuously with the musky smell of hot skin. Taking a side strand in either hand, she checked for evenness—and dropped the scissors when he suddenly closed his thighs, capturing her between them.

"You've cut enough," he said, gazing at her under lids hooded against the sun. "Tell you what. I'll tie it back for the party. Just for you."

"Thanks a lot." Her gratitude was less than heartfelt. "Let me loose."

"I wonder."

"What?"

"Whether you should pay your penalty now." He circled her waist and rested his hands in the small of her back.

"The statute of limitations has run out," she said.

"I don't think so."

He was squeezing so insistently, she felt tipsy.

"I'm sure this state has laws about that." She was embarrassed at how weak her protest was.

"So does the Azrat tribe."

"Who are these Azrats?"

"Let me tell you a little secret."

He pulled her down on his lap and whispered in her ear.

"You didn't!" she said, giggling.

"Sad to say, I did. I made it up."

"Your grandfather must hate that name."

"He isn't too happy that his only heir is walking around with my father's name, either. That's why I spiced it up a bit."

"You just made the word up? It doesn't mean a thing?"

"It means, love, Africa is my home, and that's where I intend to live. Unless my grandfather accepts that, we're not going to be able to chuck all the baggage from the past."

"Do you want to?" She had to get away from him before she literally melted at his feet.

"I thought I did."

He stood, helping her to her feet, but didn't attempt to claim his kiss.

When he left, leaving her to sweep up hair and return the borrowed items, she tried to tell herself she was irritated because he didn't help to clean up.

But she knew her disappointment went much deeper, and much closer to her heart.

To JANE'S SURPRISE, Luke didn't give her any static about going to the party the next night. He met her in the living room, on time and resplendent in new pale gray trousers and a tailored white shirt, the cotton so fine it was semitransparent. True to his word, his hair was neatly tied back with a leather thong.

"Very nice," he'd said in a low, sexy drawl, openly looking her over when she came downstairs in Kim's white halter dress. "Very nice indeed."

"It's my sister's," Jane said, sure she was blushing all the way to her toes at his reaction. "I didn't even realize she put it in my bag until I got here."

"Don't do that, love." He stepped close and brushed a tendril of dark hair from her cheek.

"Don't do what?"

"Don't be so self-deprecating. Don't give your sister credit. That dress is gorgeous because you're in it."

"Let's go," she said, knowing she should thank him for the compliment but unnerved by his minilecture.

Luke drove at a snail's pace, by his standards, so he wouldn't miss the palatial home hidden away in the hills on the outskirts of Sedona. When they got there, he gave the place high marks for ostentation with its ornate iron gate, impressive desert landscaping and stained-glass windows, but he could think of much better places to take Janie in her sensational backless dress. The white set off the sleek, lightly tanned skin of her back and arms, and the short, flared skirt whirled tantalizingly above long, shapely legs, making it hard to concentrate on anything else.

She was nervous about mingling with Rupert's snooty friends, and nothing he could say was likely to reassure her. He might do more harm than good if he said what he was thinking: every woman there was sure to envy her; she had the kind of inner radiance that comes along maybe once in a generation.

"If we're not having fun, we'll leave," he said instead.

"We can't do that! Your grandfather—"

"We'll play it by ear."

Somehow he'd get through this evening without confessing how he really felt about her. He'd thought of little else recently, but he couldn't make one plus one equal two. Following a hard hat into remote areas of Africa was no life for her. Taking over his grandfather's company was akin to a life sentence for him. They'd end up like his own parents had: apart and miserable.

His father had never recovered. His mother had built a new life, but her letters had told him how much she missed her son. Luke's loyalty to his father and love of Africa had made him refuse to join her after she remarried. To her credit, she understood and did the best she could to keep in touch. He regretted the separation, especially since her life had been so short, but this lingering pain made him even more determined not to pursue Jane.

He let a valet park the Ferrari, then put his hand under Jane's elbow and steeled himself to begin partying.

"You must be Rupert's grandson," a scrawny woman in a silvery, space-suit sort of jumpsuit said, descending on them as they walked under a two-ton chandelier into the main room at the front. "I'm Amelia Wellington."

"Call me Luke. This is my friend, Jane Grant," he said, almost able to see a cloud of perfume condensing around their hostess. He liked a nice subtle scent, but the natural fragrance of Jane's skin was more appealing to him than anything that came in an overpriced bottle.

"Miss Grant, a pleasure," the woman said with the automatic charm of someone who'd extended the same welcome a thousand times. "The buffet is set up poolside. You can go out those doors and to your right. Later, I'd just love to hear all about Africa, Luke."

As they walked toward the pool, the tiny frown on Jane's face made him even more reluctant to hobnob with Rupert's friends. In her scene-stealing dress, Jane wasn't going to be a success with the women, but he'd expected testosterone levels to shoot up like geysers when the men saw her. But, he soon discovered, not even lechery was enough to liven up the middle-aged and older crowd of successful bores. Janie never lacked for someone to make small talk with, but after a couple of hours her smile was almost as pasted on as their hostess's.

He managed to corner her when she was momentarily alone.

"I guess your grandfather couldn't make it," she said sympathetically.

"Doubt he ever intended to. It's the Azrat way of learning to swim. Throw the kid in the water and watch while he swims or goes under."

"You're no kid."

He was glad to see real warmth in her smile.

"And Rupert's no Azrat. He's just too smart to put up with a whole evening of dull chitchat," he said less sharply.

"The buffet was nice, especially the seafood," she said to change the subject.

"You ate one shrimp and half a cracker."

"I didn't know you were counting."

"I wasn't, but watching you is the only entertainment here. Do you think I've been sufficiently introduced into polite society?"

"Luke, it's not even dark. Mr. Wellington went on and on about how terrific the grounds look when the lights come on."

"What this affair needs is livening up," he said thoughtfully.

"Whatever you're thinking, don't. You said we'd leave if the party wasn't fun."

"It will be. Leave it to me, Janie."

He walked over to one of the white-jacketed waiters clearing away the buffet while she warily watched his every move. So far, nothing catastrophic. After a lengthy conversation Luke seemed to be returning to the other guests when he stopped by one of the tables and lifted a bright red-and-yellow-striped umbrella out of the well in the center. Before she could guess what he was planning, he separated the long pole, tossed aside the umbrella part and recruited two dazed waiters to hold the ends.

"Limbo, everyone!"

A boom box materialized, blasting away at enough decibels to bring the police if someone played it that loud in her neighborhood.

"The best sport takes the first turn," Luke announced, walking up to a woman with improbably black hair piled high on her head.

"I haven't done the limbo since I was a Girl Scout," she protested, looking for support from her bald, slightly paunchy husband, who definitely wasn't amused.

Luke took her hand, and she followed him over to the pole like one of the Pied Piper's victims.

"Show 'em, Maggie," one of the livelier men called out.

She threw her head back theatrically, wiggled hips encased in a midthigh white satin skirt and went under the pole with a spate of giggles.

The game was on. Jane watched with horror—and amusement—while their hostess gyrated her hips and wiggled under, followed by a plump, rusty-haired man who sent the bar flying.

"If there are more savages like him in the jungle, I'm definitely going to Africa on my next trip," a high-maintenance blonde said, coming up beside Jane as Luke finished his turn at the lowest level so far.

"One of the big thrills is a wildebeest ride," Luke said, overhearing the woman's comment and coming over.

"I love exotic rides," the woman purred.

Jane wanted to kick her cosmetically enhanced and aerobically conditioned rear end when Luke went down on one knee, his back toward the blonde, and ordered her to hop aboard. She did, pulling the thong out of his hair as he pranced around the pool with her on his shoulders, a rap beat blaring out of the boom box.

Jane backed away from the action, wanting to be part of it but too conscious of her role as Luke's keeper.

"Oh, boy," she muttered when limbo madness gave way to a conga line snaking between tables led, of course, by Wild-Man Azrat.

He was a rip-roaring success; she just wanted to go home. He dropped away from the revelers and came over to her, taking her hand and trying to get her to catch hold of the last person in the line.

"I'd really rather go home." She meant her real home, but for tonight she'd settle for her temporary quarters.

"Janie, love—"

"Stop calling me love!"

"Miss Jane Grant, the party is only starting to warm up," he said. "Please stay."

"If you won't leave, let me have the keys."

"Have you ever driven a Ferrari?"

She hadn't, and she couldn't imagine facing Mr. Cox if she got the slightest dent on a car like that.

"Never mind."

The blond jockey came over, no doubt hoping for another ride—and not necessarily around the pool.

"I'll get home on my own," Jane said.

"I'm leaving now," a dark-haired man with a bolo

tie and cowboy boots said. "Be glad to drop you off."

Never accept rides from strangers, she'd always been taught, but she'd seen her rescuer talking to practically everyone there. It was much more likely that she'd kill Luke than this stranger would turn out to be a serial killer.

Somewhat to her surprise, her benefactor didn't come on to her, didn't ask to be invited in for a nightcap and didn't even seem interested in talking.

Less than a half hour after he dropped her off, she discovered why.

She picked up the shrilly ringing phone reluctantly, afraid anyone calling late at night had to be the bearer of bad news.

This caller was bad news personified.

"Miss Grant, I don't like what I heard about the party. Some pretty important people were looking my grandson over—three board members were in attendance. His antics could make it damn near impossible to get him approved as the next CEO."

"You weren't there. I mean, the party isn't even over, sir."

"I got a full report on Luke's abominable behavior. I expected better guidance from you, young lady. You're seriously jeopardizing your future with this company."

Why was she so gullible? The Good Samaritan who gave her a ride home must have been a spy for her boss!

"This is your last chance," he went on. "Your job is to civilize my grandson and keep him in line. I expect you to be the one keeping tabs on him."

She hung up, feeling two inches high. Miss Polk

was an amateur compared to her boss, when it came
to chastising the hired help.

Jane was mad enough to throw a tantrum—if she
knew how. Kim was the one who used to have
healthy outlets like raging and screaming. She was
practical Jane, always ready to be reasonable, logical
and sensible. Luke probably thought she was dull,
dull, dull. And she was, she thought, dragging herself
to bed.

Finally, sometime after 2:00 a.m., she dozed off.


"WAKE UP, sleepyhead. This is becoming a habit."

His voice was soft and teasing. He'd retied his
hair, but his shirt was hanging out, unbuttoned down
the front.

"Your grandfather called me." Even asleep she'd
stayed mad. "He had a spy at the party, not to mention three board members who would have to approve your appointment as CEO."

"Nice of him to warn us. He didn't fire you, did
he?" He wasn't faking his concern.

"Not yet, and I'm going to quit anyway as soon
as I can. Maybe if you apologize…"

"Apologize! To whom? For what? All I did was
liven up a deadly dull affair. I'd rather hang out with
a bunch of hyenas waiting for leftovers than go
through the first part of that evening again."

"What a colorful way of putting it," she said
dryly, getting out of bed to confront him. "You certainly seemed to be having a good time when I left."

"I make my own good times, but this isn't one of
them, Jane. If you don't mind, I'm going to bed
now."

"Don't let me stop you," she said.

"I don't suppose you want to tuck me in again?" he asked, his anger dissolving faster than the ice cubes at Jackrabbit Acres.

"What's in it for me?" She tried, but didn't succeed, in bantering with the same good humor he showed.

"That's really what it's all about, isn't it? What's in it for everybody—my grandfather, his board of directors, the company minions, Miss Polk. I'm just a pawn in Rupert's power ploys."

"Maybe you should go to bed," she said, hurt by his outburst.

"I didn't mean you, Jane. I saw Rupert blackmail you into being my keeper. But you don't have to stay with the company. I sure don't intend to hook up with it."

"Then why stay and play your grandfather's game?" she asked angrily.

"Damned if I know, unless it's this."

He pulled her against him and kissed her so emphatically she gasped. Reflex took over, and she wrapped her arms around him, ready for the next kiss and the next, returning them as his hands moved over her shoulders and back, hard and persuasive and exciting.

Things were moving too fast; she couldn't let down her guard and fall for a man who didn't have a place for her in his life—or his heart.

She pushed against his chest with her palms, knowing she couldn't break free unless he let her and half hoping he wouldn't.

"Sorry, I'm not interested," she lied in a husky, broken whisper.

"Neither am I."

He released her and moved swiftly away. She couldn't bear to watch his retreat.

# 9

SHE'D BEEN STAYING at Rupert Cox's elegant summer home for only two weeks, but it felt like two years. And her reason for being there was absurd: clean up his grandson's act. Much to her sorrow, she'd never met anyone less in need of transforming than Luke. Far from being the kind of bad boy who spelled disaster for long-term relationships, he was considerate, self-confident, intelligent and complex, nothing like the shallow men who had let her down in the past.

Worse, he was devastatingly attractive: tall, strong, distinctive and charismatic. She thought about him constantly, recognizing her emotion for what it was—love.

Who knew it could hurt so much to care for someone? He was the perfect man except for one small fact: his goal was to get back to Africa as soon as possible, a trip that didn't include her.

Would she go with him if he asked?

Maybe. Probably.

The way she felt now, she'd gladly live in a jungle tree house to be with him, but she knew herself too well to pretend they would live happily ever after. She'd miss Kim like crazy, and, worse, she'd feel guilty for breaking up their little family.

What Jane wanted most was a family of her own:

kids and a husband who would stay around to be a good father. Nothing Luke had said about his job or lifestyle suggested he'd ever be content in one place. The tree house didn't seem so romantic when she tried to imagine children in it.

Last night at the party, he'd gone too far. He'd made her look really ineffectual, at least in the eyes of Rupert's spy. But Luke was a full-grown, strong-minded man. How could anyone expect her coaching to make him executive material? She was trapped. Even if she hated her job—and she was beginning to—she wanted to leave it with the good recommendations she deserved.

Before she had a chance to go to breakfast, she got a phone call from Miss Polk.

"Really, Jane, Mr. Cox isn't at all happy. Do you need me to come replace you there?"

"No, I'm sure Luke was only trying to liven up the party."

Miss Polk cleared her throat skeptically.

"He was disappointed his grandfather wasn't there," Jane said.

She was curious herself why Mr. Cox wasn't spending more time with Luke.

"That's none of our affair."

Of course, she meant it was none of Jane's business.

No more fooling around, Azrat, Jane thought, after Miss Polk ended her lecture and hung up.

It was Luke's fault she was stuck in Sedona. The least he could do was cooperate. She psyched herself up to read him the riot act.

Practically foaming at the mouth in her eagerness to let him know what she thought of his stunts, she hurried to the dining room. Mrs. Horning was there, clearing the remains of Luke's breakfast.

"He's gone?" Jane asked without remembering to say good morning.

The housekeeper's confirmation was unnecessary as Jane heard the familiar sound of Luke's car retreating down the driveway.

LUKE DROVE without a destination, relying on the high-power Ferrari to distract his thoughts. He knew he was in deep trouble when driving didn't give him any pleasure. It was his grandfather's fault, of course, but he had grudging admiration, tinged with amusement, for the old man's cunning. How better to manipulate a reluctant heir apparent than assigning him a beautiful, desirable woman as his watchdog? The trouble was, Rupert's ploy had worked too well.

He'd done it again: pulled a dumb stunt to put her off. The party had been deadly dull; he wasn't sorry about livening it up. His regret was he hadn't danced with Jane, hadn't held her in his arms, hadn't made love to her.

He groaned and pulled off the road where parking was provided so people could stop and enjoy a sparkling stream. This early in the morning the site was deserted. He got out and sat on a big rock, skipping stones in the water, at a loss what to do about Jane.

Several hours later he arrived back at the house, no easier in his mind about her but still convinced a romantic relationship was a red flag for them.

"Hello," he said, finding her in the office scowling at a fax.

"These are for you."

She stood and thrust a wad of papers into his hand.

"Thank you."

He thought of depositing them in the waste bin, but she didn't look in the mood for theatrical gestures. In fact, she looked steamed.

"Don't smirk," she warned heatedly. "From now on I'm getting tough."

She was so earnest, so emphatic, so desirable, he wanted to take her in his arms and tell her to forget the nonsense about molding him to fit the corporate image. Instead, he did something bad. He laughed.

"I mean it, Luke. I still can't believe your grandfather had a spy at the party."

"The chap who drove you home?" he asked, feigning indifference when actually he'd been tormented by jealousy after she left, an exceedingly rare state of mind for him.

"Yes, and this morning Miss Polk was on her high horse."

"Uncomfortable position, always in a stew trying to control other people's lives," he observed mildly, wanting to wipe away the disapproval on her face with long, hot kisses.

"I wish you'd go back to your bridge building and get this over with!"

Her angry outburst only made him long to hold her in his arms even more. She was dressed in white shorts and a sleeveless pink top that paled beside the flush in her cheeks. He didn't want her to be upset, but what could he say that wouldn't mislead her?

"There's nothing I'd like more," he lied, knowing he loved the hot, arid beauty of this corner of the world almost as much as he loved his homeland.

"Then what's keeping you here?" she asked.

"I gave my word," he said dejectedly, hating his

rash promise to become CEO of the company if he decided to stay in the States.

"You're not keeping it! You're not even considering your grandfather's offer. Why don't you leave and stop—"

"Stop what?" he asked when she turned her back and seemed at a loss for words.

"Stop acting like an idiot! Behave yourself!"

There was no way to defend himself without telling her how he really felt. What he wanted to say was best said holding her against him, hugging her, punctuating words with long, sweet kisses.

"You might stop imitating Polk," he said instead as he walked away, leaving because he was as angry with himself as he was with her.


JANE HEARD the car roar away for a second time, and her throat ached with the effort of not crying. For just a moment she'd seen a warmth in his eyes that made her heart race, or maybe it was only wishful thinking on her part. Couldn't he see that she was his best chance for happiness, that they belonged together?

"You're an idiot," she said to herself, wondering why she didn't just leave, but knowing the reason had nothing to do with her job.

She waited with the patience of a charging rhino to see if Luke would return for dinner. By four in the afternoon she felt as if she'd been waiting a year.

She was in the office, trying to occupy herself by arranging paper clips and rubber bands in the desk drawer, when the phone rang.

"Janie." Luke's voice was oddly reserved. "I have to ask a big favor."

"Your humble servant has only to hear to obey," she said sarcastically. An afternoon of pacing and fretting had fueled her anger until she was ready to take him on with boxing gloves.

"I need you to post bail for me."

"Post bail?" She was so stunned, she forgot about being angry. "Why? Where are you?"

"I'm in jail in a place called Coppertown. Do you know it?"

"Yes, but why… What did you do?"

"Seems I was driving a bit fast. The local law officers took umbrage with my attitude. No sporting blood here. Didn't help that I have an international license. Did Polk have getting an Arizona license on your list or mine?"

He sounded so sheepish, she didn't rub it in that no one can get a driver's license for someone else.

"I'll have to call your grandfather to authorize bail money. Do you know how much it is?"

"No need to bother him." He sounded like a naughty little boy trying to avoid a spanking. "Just bring my traveler's checks. They're in the stand by the bed."

"If I do this, will you promise to behave and do everything I tell you for the rest of your visit?"

She thought it was worth a try, but there was dead silence on the other end of the line.

"Please let me talk to Willard," he requested in a strained voice.

"Oh, never mind. I'll come."

She couldn't let her boss's irascible grandson— and the man she loved—go to someone else for help. He'd probably fallen prey to a speed trap, but, judging by the rides she'd taken with him, she had no doubt about his guilt. It might be good for him to be locked up for the night. How bad could the Coppertown jail be?

She remembered an old movie she'd seen where a tourist was railroaded for an innocuous offense and sent to a chain gang on a prison farm. However unlikely it was that Luke would end up in orange coveralls and shackles, she couldn't help being worried about him.

The traveler's checks were easy to find, but the rest of her rescue mission hit a snag. Her car battery, left to bake under the hot summer sun without being driven enough to charge it, staged a major rebellion. It was soon clear she wasn't going anywhere in her car.

Willard was obliging, but he had a problem.

"My wife's mother is poorly. Miss Polk said to go ahead and run her down to Mesa for as long as she's needed there. I promised we'd leave as soon as supper is ready."

"I'm sorry about her mother," Jane said sympathetically. "If we leave right now, could you take me to Coppertown, then go to Mesa? There's no need for Wilma to fix dinner."

A few hours later the Hornings somewhat reluctantly left her on the dusty main street of an off-the-beaten-path tourist town. She'd had time to think about whether to bail out a man who thought he could flout all the rules.

She was within sight of the small brick building that served as police headquarters and, she surmised, also had holding cells for minor offenders, but she'd also noticed a number of tourist facilities on the way into town. Squaring her shoulders, she walked away from the jail and toward the nearest bed-and-breakfast. She was hungry, tired from a near-sleepless night and sick of playing nanny to Rupert Cox's rebellious grandson. Let him cool his heels.

The bed-and-breakfast had been a saloon and brothel in the rip-roaring days when mining flourished in the surrounding hills. The current owners had preserved the flavor of the Old West on the main floor, keeping the original bar and some tables in the front room while converting the rear into private living quarters. Upstairs, her room, reasonably priced because it was the off-season for tourists, was small but cozy with electrified replicas of gas lamps on the wall, a brass bedstead and a dresser with a pitcher and bowl for ornamental purposes, not for washing up as originally intended. The bathroom was down the hall, but the room was pleasant with colorful cotton-appliqué baskets embroidered on a cream-colored spread.

She wondered if Luke would have to sleep on an iron slab with no mattress.

*He deserves it,* she thought without much conviction, then consoled herself by walking down the street to a family-style restaurant in what had once been the town bank. She had a huge spinach salad with real bacon and fresh hot bread brought to the table on a little wooden cutting board. She wondered what prisoners in the town jail were fed, probably institutional fare like beans and franks or macaroni and cheese. She didn't like to think of Luke going hungry, but he didn't seem to be a fussy eater.

She went to bed really early, sinking down on the soft mattress and taking deep breaths to relax, but her mind wouldn't turn off. Luke deserved to stew in jail, but she couldn't erase the vision of a dank little cell with him huddled on an iron cot while rats scurried around his dinner tray on the cold concrete floor.

If he called his grandfather or Miss Polk, would one of them rescue him? Somehow, she doubted it. They'd probably want him to be punished a while. Was she acting like one of them, lying on a comfy, if overly soft, bed while Luke was in a miserable lockup, maybe sharing space with really mean criminals?

She rolled across the double bed, trying to find a good sleeping position, but she couldn't have been more wide-awake.

Darn it! She kept thinking about Luke driving her to the hospital after Kim's accident. He'd been compassionate and caring when she needed help. In fact, when he wasn't thwarting her every move and driving her crazy, he was one of the kindest, most considerate men she'd ever met.

Her eyes felt glued open; she was getting more exercise tossing and turning on the bed than she would in an aerobics workout. How long had she been trying to sleep? She looked at the light filtering through the window blinds; it wasn't even dark yet. No wonder she was wide-awake in spite of her fatigue.

"Oh, shoot!" she said aloud, finally giving in.

She felt too guilty to sleep. She couldn't leave Luke in jail. A few minutes later she was dressed and on her way to fetch him.

THE JAIL WASN'T quite the chamber of horrors she'd been imagining. The lone officer on duty was presiding over an orderly little office with the ambience of a drivers' licensing bureau. He went through a rear door and brought Luke, unchained and probably unrepentant, to the desk to sign traveler's checks for his release.

"What took you so long?" he asked her as the officer did some paperwork.

"Let's just get your car and leave." She wasn't ready for explanations.

"I'm sorry, ma'am. I'm not authorized to release the vehicle. You'll have to come back after eight tomorrow morning."

"But he paid the fine."

"Yes, ma'am, but you'll have to claim the vehicle in the morning."

He exaggerated his drawl, and she suspected he was enjoying his authority—the power to do nothing.

"Let's go," Luke said, taking her arm.

"But he has no right to—"

"We'll collect the car in the morning," Luke said firmly, leading her out to the pavement.

"They can't keep your car," she argued.

"Seems they can for now."

"You could thank me for coming," she said.

"Isn't it part of your job?"

"I should've left you in jail!"

"I thought you were going to. What took you so long?" he repeated.

"I wonder why I bothered coming at all."

"Where's your car?" He looked in all directions.

"In Sedona," she had to admit. "My battery is dead."

"How did you get here?"

"Mr. Horning. He had to go to Mesa because his wife's mother is sick."

"So we're stranded here. Why spring me? At least I had a place to sleep, albeit not five-star."

"I'm overwhelmed by your gratitude."

She'd been avoiding his gaze, but she looked up now to meet his eyes, weak with relief knowing he was all right. How was she going to feel when he went back to Africa to sleep in tents or huts or who-knew-what with marauding lions and awful croco-diles just waiting to make a meal of him?

"We'd better find a room, I guess," Luke said.

He put his arm around her shoulders, making her feel protected and cherished, an illusion she couldn't afford to enjoy. She pulled away, her emotions too fragile to risk getting any closer to a man who was going to leave.

"I have one at a bed-and-breakfast. Maybe you can get a room there, too."

"Let's give it a try," he said cheerfully.

It was a no-go, the owner informed them. All the other rooms were taken. If they wanted to share hers, it would be twelve dollars extra, including the break-fast.

"No, that won't—" Jane started to say as Luke was handing over the extra money.

"How will you list this on your expense ac-count?" he teased, ignoring her protests about shar-ing a room. "You could call it a field trip."

"You could get a room somewhere else."

"Do you want me out on the dark streets in this wild frontier town?" he asked, grinning like a lottery winner.

She fumbled with the lock, then flounced into the room. It seemed smaller than when she'd left it.

"You can sleep on the floor," she informed him.

"No way, love. Synthetic carpets make me itch."

"Well, I'm not sleeping on the floor." She looked at the lone chair, straight-backed with only a thin cushion covering the wooden seat.

"We'll share the bed—platonically, of course," he said.

He sounded so matter-of-fact she wanted to shake him.

"When horses grow horns!"

"Then you'll have unicorns, won't you?" he asked with mild amusement. "Any chance of a shower?"

"Down the hall," she said crossly, trying to conceal the excitement pounding through her by being crabby.

"No need to wait up for me," he said, still maddeningly cheerful. "I'll just take the key. You won't use the dead bolt to lock me out, will you?"

She could imagine the scene he'd create: banging on the door, shouting witticisms, disturbing the whole place.

"I'll be sleeping when you get back," she said, pretending to be indifferent, as he left the room.

How could she sleep with him and not *sleep* with him? She couldn't do this. She absolutely couldn't do this.

He was fast, too fast. Before she could come up with a convincing reason for throwing him out, he was back.

"Luke, I don't want to sleep with you." She chose

the direct way, awkward as it was, because he might not want to do more than really sleep.

"I took a cold shower," he said glumly, still toweling his water-darkened hair.

To his credit, he'd redressed in his khaki shorts and body-hugging tank top, the cotton knit clinging damply to his chest. She would need a shower of frozen slush to eradicate what she was thinking.

"It's not the busy season for tourists. Maybe I can find a room somewhere else," she said.

"Bad idea, love. I won't have you walking the streets of a strange town by yourself."

"Then you go."

"No, we're rational, trustworthy adults. I give you my word I won't take advantage of the situation."

She knew how honorable he was when it came to keeping promises. She had to believe he'd keep his word about this, but could she trust herself?

"All right," she reluctantly agreed, suddenly seized by a compelling urge to brush her teeth. She grabbed the small bag she'd brought in case she decided to leave Luke in jail overnight and left the room.

When she returned, intending to sleep in the clothes she'd worn all day, Luke was in bed, sprawled out squarely in the middle, the sheet blanketing him up to his chin. She had her choice of six inches on his right or six inches on his left.

"There's no room for me," she whispered, hoping his closed eyes meant he was sleeping, although how she'd roll him over to make room for herself, she didn't know.

"Here, I'll get off your half."

He sat, letting the sheet fall, revealing his bare shoulders and chest.

"You're not wearing anything!"

"Don't look so horrified. You saw me in the pool."

"Tell me you're wearing your nice new—"

"The old ones suit me better."

She crawled into bed, wishing she hadn't asked. Especially she wished her imagination didn't work so well.

BY THE TIME the morning light was seeping through the blinds, Luke had to wonder if he'd gotten two hours' sleep. The bed felt stuffed with cotton balls and sloped downward in the center. He'd spent most of the night trying to cling to the far edge, exerting every ounce of self-control to keep his word. He'd never done anything harder in his life, lying there listening to Jane's soft breathing and aching to show her how he really felt.

Now, after a night of torture, he might still give himself away. She'd rolled against him—how could she not in this sorry excuse for a bed—and her warm form was pressed against his backside, liquid lightning shooting through him, testing his self-control to the max.

He felt her stir and held his breath, not wanting their contact to end even though it was making him miserable.

"You didn't stay on your side," she protested sleepily, waking up enough to realize she was on his side. "Oh, I'm sorry."

"The bed dips in the middle," he said magnanimously, suffering even more as she tried to wiggle away from him.

"I'll get up," she said.

She'd rolled away, but not far enough. The way he felt about her, he wasn't sure an ocean would put enough space between them to get her out of his head.

"It's still too early to get the car," he murmured. "Sorry I crowded you."

"Come back, just for a while."

"Luke, it's not a good idea."

She wanted to; he could hear it in her soft tone and sense it in the way she stiffened, still only inches from him.

"We'll just lie here for a few minutes," he promised.

"That's what the boys used to say in high school," she protested weakly.

"Did you believe them?"

"I wanted to, but I didn't."

She wasn't talking about schoolboys in her past, he was sure.

He rolled on his side, snuggling against her fantastic backside, wishing she'd taken off her shorts. He draped one arm across her shoulders, not resting it there but trailing his arm downward, over her waist to her hip. Touching her thigh took his breath away. It was sleek and smooth and warm—everything he'd imagined and more.

Had he ever wanted any woman so badly? He had to inch away to keep from parting her between her thighs and ruining the magic that was building between them.

It was sheer torture, but at the same time it was

so deeply satisfying to hold her in his arms, he gladly honored his promise because it meant more time to love her with his heart.

She turned lazily onto her back, and he desperately wanted to put his hand under her rumpled shirt and caress her breasts, obviously freed from the constraints of a bra. He felt shaky just seeing her delicate nipples hardening under the soft cotton.

"Luke."

"What, Janie, love?"

She was quiet for so long, he thought she might have gone back to sleep.

"We should get up," she murmured at last.

"I know." He took her hand, bringing it to his bristly chin and touching the tips of her fingers with his tongue.

He closed his eyes and drew her little finger between his lips, gently suckling it. When she pulled it away, she rested her hand on his chest, touching his nipple with the moistened fingertip.

How was he going to live apart from her? He couldn't ruin her life the way his mother's had been ruined, and he couldn't stay without honoring his promise to take over his grandfather's company if he decided to live in the States.

He sat up abruptly, knowing they had to stop or he risked doing the unthinkable: hurting Jane.

# *10*

JANE WAS SO CAUTIOUS driving the leased Ferrari, she let a battered pickup pulling a horse van pass her. Luke snorted his disapproval every time an old clunker cut in front of them, but he didn't criticize her driving. In fact, she was still amazed he hadn't given her any argument about not driving himself until he had an Arizona license.

Except for a few questions about Kim, he was quiet on the way home, and she wasn't up to small talk, except to say her sister was doing fine. Probably better than she was. She'd made a terrible mistake getting a room at the bed-and-breakfast, then letting Luke share it with her.

He'd held her in his arms and rejected her. He didn't want her. If he had, he would have found her the most willing partner possible.

She kept telling herself it was much better to find out now, rather than have him leave after making love, but there was a hollow ache where her heart used to be. She wanted him in her bed and in her life forever, not just one night.

Dummy, she admonished herself. *You never had a chance. He's the boss's wayward grandson. You're just his watchdog. Get on with your life!*

That meant getting on with her job, and her current assignment was a real stinker. She wanted to play the woman scorned and storm out of Luke's life. Unfortunately, or maybe fortunately, her pragmatic side insisted she do the stiff-upper-lip bit and hang on to her job until something better came along.

So she drove Luke into Sedona and waited while he took his driver's test. At least she had the satisfaction afterward of hearing him bluster because he'd missed four questions.

"You did get a license," she said mildly.

"That's not the point! The test must have been written by a chimpanzee. It didn't take into consideration road conditions or emergency situations. Take number eleven—"

"Do you want to drive home?" she interrupted, dangling the keys in front of his face.

"Then there was the one about turn signals," he fumed as he reached for the key ring.

She let him rant, realizing his anger was targeted at the bureaucratic test as a substitute for what was really bothering him. She sighed, knowing he was deliberately shutting her out.

THE NEXT FEW DAYS passed without incident. That alone was enough to make Jane nervous about what Luke might do next. At the house, he kept appointments with people from the company, not giving them any trouble. He didn't seem to mind talking to the production engineers and designers, but he said very little to her. He was withdrawn and often absent when he wasn't involved in business meetings.

Jane didn't get a single fax from Miss Polk for three days running, but she was sure Luke was far from "civilized." Maybe he was only biding his

time until he could honorably leave the country—
and her.

As crazy as he drove her with his antics, she
wasn't sure what to make of the new, subdued Luke.
Unfortunately, his outward changes didn't at all af-
fect how she felt about the inner man. He was everything she'd ever wanted: wild and adventurous,
but gentle and caring.

Even if he did feel something for her, his life and
heart were halfway around the world. No matter how
much she loved him, there was no way she could
compete with that.

Plus, she had worries that had nothing to do with
what he did or didn't feel about her. His big public
debut was coming up. Rupert was throwing a soiree
to introduce his grandson to the company's principal
shareholders. The other party had only been a dress
rehearsal; this was the one that counted.

Now she knew how a shipbuilder must feel the
day his vessel was launched. Would Luke sink or
swim in his grandfather's eyes? As a precaution, she
spent her spare time reading help wanted ads in the
*Phoenix Monitor.*

The evening arrived as all dates with destiny do,
or so Jane thought as she put on her modest little
black dress for the second time since arriving in Sedona. She could go in her bathrobe for all the attention she was likely to attract. This was Luke's night;
a lot of people would be sizing him up, thinking of
profit and loss statements or stock prices. He was
meeting the money people, the ones who counted
most. She didn't have a clue what they'd think of
him.

One consolation was that the party was being held

at a prestigious resort tucked away among the red rocks of Sedona. She wouldn't have a long trip down the mountain with Luke, sitting by his side and wishing the ride could go on forever.

She was waiting near the bottom of the spiral stairs, hoping he was nearly ready so they wouldn't get a black mark for tardiness. She looked up when she heard his door, and her heartbeat accelerated as he came down the stairs.

His new silk-blend midnight blue tuxedo had looked dashing on the hanger, but on him it was dynamite. If she hadn't seen the scruffy Luke, she would have thought he was born to wear exquisitely styled formal wear. She silently thanked the tailor for producing such elegance without a fitting, but she knew the perfection was Luke more than the tux. He looked so splendid and refined, even his grandfather shouldn't mind his long hair held back by a narrow black ribbon.

"Do I pass muster?" he asked, grinning at the approval he saw on her face. He was wearing the monkey suit for Jane, and her expression when she saw it made even the stiff shirt worthwhile.

"You look wonderful!"

He loved the way she wasn't coy or reticent about expressing her feelings. In fact, he loved everything about her, not the least her ability to look both sexy and regal in her little black dress. He desperately longed to unzip the long back closure and kiss the creamy skin under it.

Since he'd held her in his arms after his jail stay, she hadn't been out of his thoughts. He wanted her so badly, the longing was a constant pain. Was it possible? Could he find a way for them to be together? He was weary of his grandfather's manipulations, but Jane was confusing his thought processes, clouding his judgment, making him wonder if he could ever get her out of his system.

They were walking toward the front door when the whine of the fax machine caught their attention.

"Ignore it," he advised, fed up with electronic micromanagement.

"I'd better not. It might be something I'm supposed to take to the party."

"I thought you were supposed to take me," he said dryly, but he accompanied her into the office.

He was the one to pick up the first sheet, frowning as he scanned it.

"What is it?"

"Good question," he said angrily. "My guess is, it's a copy of a press release."

She reached for it, but he didn't give her any of the three pages until he'd read them all.

"What the hell is this?" he demanded.

"I can't read through the back of the paper. At least show it to me."

She read the first page and looked up at him with beseeching eyes. "I didn't know anything about this."

"Aren't you going to congratulate the new CEO of Cox Corporation?" he asked, too furious at his grandfather's high-handed tactics to spare her his wrath.

"It says he's retiring. Did you know that?" she asked.

"Apparently I'm the last person to know a lot of things. How deep are you into this conspiracy?"

"I'm not! It's the first I've heard of it!"

"You can't possibly be as innocent as you seem," he said, lashing out.

"If you think—"

"If my grandfather thinks I'll be pressured by premature publicity, he still has a lot to learn. The only agreement I have with the old pirate is to stay six weeks. As far as I'm concerned, this tripe negates our deal whether it's been released to the press yet or not."

"What do you mean?"

"I mean, have a good time at the party. I'm not going!"

"Luke!"

She watched him storm out, then hurried after him to no avail.

Why, oh why, hadn't she thought to steal the man's car keys?

He was getting into the Ferrari when she burst through the door.

"Don't expect me to bail you out again!" she yelled.

He made a grand prix start and roared out of sight as despair washed over her.

Somehow she got to the party alone, her newly recharged battery performing better than the missing guest of honor. Considering Luke's state of mind, it was probably best if he headed straight for the airport.

How on earth was she going to tell his grandfather that Luke wouldn't be there?

Rupert Cox was holding court in the intimidating grand ballroom of the resort, surrounded by beautiful people who made Jane feel like one of Cinderella's stepsisters.

"Mr. Cox, can I speak to you, please?"

She must have looked as terrified as she felt. He took her arm and led her to a window alcove where she could deliver her message of doom in relative privacy.

"Sir, uh, well—"

"Spit it out, Miss Grant."

"Luke isn't coming, sir."

She'd never actually seen thunderclouds on a human face—until now.

"He'd better have a damn good reason."

She was going to be blamed no matter what excuse she gave. She jumped on the one least likely to result in her job being publicly terminated on the spot.

"He's feeling sick."

She was the one most likely to become ill.

Rupert wasn't pleased, but at least she'd given him a plausible excuse to relay to his guests. He wasn't going to can her on the spot.

He went to explain things, and she was planning her escape when the worst possible thing happened.

Luke showed up.

He walked toward the center of the huge room, conversations dying out in his wake. Gone was every hallmark of a civilized man. Clad in ragged shorts, he was bare-chested under a shabby khaki vest. He looked as though he'd been through a dust storm, his face framed by wild, windblown hair and his feet planted in dusty hiking boots worn without socks.

If she hadn't known how little time he'd had to shed his tux and get there, she would swear he'd been drinking heavily for a long time. But it was cold fury driving him, not alcohol.

Her boss's face was mottled red with anger and

indignation, and he didn't step forward to acknowledge his grandson. Like everyone there, he watched as Luke grabbed a goblet of champagne from a waiter's tray, raised it toward his grandfather, swallowed hard and sent it crashing against a circular platform where a small orchestra was providing background music.

Two burly men in snug-fitting tuxes stepped forward, looking at Rupert for instructions.

"Throw him out," the CEO ordered.

Jane watched in horror as the security men grabbed Luke's arms and marched him out, sullen and unresisting. As she watched in shock, she heard Rupert apologizing to his guests for the "homeless" man's intrusion and explaining that his grandson had been detained by illness.

"Please enjoy yourselves," he said heartily. "We'll reschedule a party for my grandson when he's feeling more himself."

"Should we call the police about the gate-crasher?" some management type asked.

"No, just see that he stays out," Rupert ordered gruffly.

Jane had had it, but she didn't move quickly enough. The formidable older man was bearing down on her, and there was no way to avoid him.

"Miss Grant, what do you know about this?"

She shook her head dumbly. No way was he going to hear from her about Luke's reaction to the fax. Stepping between Luke and his grandfather was the surest way she knew of getting crushed.

"I have no idea," she fibbed weakly.

"Find out."

She wanted to hate her boss, but for a moment she

saw something in his face more touching than threatening. He was genuinely hurt by Luke's behavior.

"I'll do what I can, sir."

Her career at Cox was history, her heart was breaking and tears were building up like water behind a cracking dam. But old habits die hard. Luke was her job, and she was going to go down fighting.

"Please do your best, Jane," Rupert called after her.

She was outside starting her car before she realized Mr. Cox had used her first name and actually said please, but right now she couldn't think about anyone but Luke. Where would he go? She only had one good idea.

By the time she drove back to the house, parked her car and took a shortcut through the house to reach the pool, she was trembling with anger.

She found Luke furiously swimming laps in the fading light of dusk, his clothes in a chair.

"How could you do that?" she shouted when he sliced through the water near her.

"Did you enjoy the party?" he yelled back, turning and continuing to swim, forcing her to walk alongside the pool in order to be heard.

"Come out right now," she demanded. "I have to talk to you!"

"Do you?" He swam lazily to where she was standing.

"What did you accomplish with that stunt?"

He emerged from the water, stark naked but seemingly totally at ease about it. She averted her eyes and spotted a deflated vinyl mat used as a float in the pool. Not seeing anything resembling a towel, she grabbed it and threw it at him.

Smiling sardonically, he picked it up and held the floppy shield in front of him. He was ruining her life, jeopardizing her job and making her love him, but she couldn't help laughing at the makeshift loincloth.

"You can't run away from this." She wanted to say "me."

"No?" He kept his distance, water still trickling down his face.

"You may not care about your future, but you've jeopardized mine, too."

Why couldn't he see that she'd tell her boss to take a hike and work any job she could get if Luke would give the slightest indication he wanted her in his life. He was so caught up in worrying about his grandfather manipulating him, he didn't have enough sense to see happiness standing right in front of him: her.

"Do you have a message from Rupert?" he asked, bland words not quite concealing the cauldron of emotions seething just below the surface.

"Not from him, no, but maybe you're just as controlling as he is. The man wants to give you everything he's built in his life, and you keep pulling dumb stunts to put him off. Maybe you're just as heavy-handed as he is!"

She was shocked but not sorry she'd had enough nerve to challenge Luke this way. His angry expression was so like his grandfather's, she inwardly cringed but stood her ground.

"Maybe Miss Polk has competition for the job of head minion. What better way to move up in a company than by doing the boss's dirty work?"

"If that's what you think, I don't care!"

Why was he forcing her to lie when all she wanted to do was live in his orbit?

"Why don't you give up? You're not going to civilize me to Rupert's specifications."

"What will it take to get you to cooperate with me?"

"You want to make a deal?" The vinyl mat flopped against his naked thighs. "You want me to make you look good with the big boss?"

"Yes. You could start by pretending you're a gentleman instead of a savage," she snapped, her patience exhausted.

"All right. If you sleep with me."

His proposal—no, proposition—knocked the wind out of her.

"Did that already. At the bed-and-breakfast," she gasped, her throat tightening so she could hardly breathe.

She thought she'd die from the pain of wanting him and knowing he was going to walk out of her life no matter what she did—even give herself to him.

"Make love to me. That's my deal," he said more forcefully.

She was standing at the edge of a precipice. If she stepped off, would she fly or crash? She couldn't spend the rest of her life wishing she'd taken the chance.

"When and where?" she asked, determined to beat him at his own game.

"Here and now."

"Fine."

She hoped her voice sounded firm. Inside, she was shaking so hard her teeth should be rattling.

"Come here," he whispered.

She heard the vinyl mat slap the concrete, then she was in his arms without knowing which of them had moved.

His lips were cool from his swim as they closed over hers, kissing her so deeply she had to cling to his shoulders for support. She felt the grainy texture of his tongue and the ivory smoothness of his teeth as his lips moved, making the long, hard kiss an act of love.

He wanted her. Her body was electrified; her nerves were on fire. She forgot how she came to be in his embrace and returned his kisses with all her heart and soul. When he scooped her into his arms, it was a homecoming, the place where she longed to be forever.

She was lighter than he'd supposed, but the solid reality of her arms around his neck, her lips still locked on his, made him weak with longing. He raced through the house, both of them laughing in fits and starts as he navigated the spiral stairway hugging her against him.

He went to her room, hit the light switch with his elbow and lowered her to stand in front of him, her face softened by passion and even more beautiful than usual.

She was trying to see all of him without seeming to stare, a becoming modesty he found endearing. He saw happiness and anticipation on her face, along with a touch of awe that flattered him immensely. With downcast eyes, her lids were delicate flower petals, and her slightly parted lips were temptation incarnate. He hoped she wanted him at least a fraction as much as he wanted her.

"Trust me," he said with a stab of conscience because he was only thinking of the present, not what would follow when he left.

"Can I?"

She stood, unresisting as he unzipped her dress and lifted it over her head. Underneath she was wearing a black nylon slip, the lacy hem clinging to the fullness of her thighs.

Beneath the tan line on her chest, her breasts swelled over the confines of black lace. In his imagination he'd caressed them, kissed them, suckled until her nipples were hard under his tongue. The reality of actually touching her on top of her lingerie was far more wonderful. He felt undeserving but blessed. He kissed her with gratitude, then with love, engulfing her in his arms and never wanting to let go.

His body was sending him one message; his heart another. He needed to be inside her, but he wanted to be part of her forever. How could he possibly make love to her only once or only twice or only four times a day until he left? And he was leaving, of that he was sure.

He couldn't do it. If he made love to her now, he'd never be able to go.

He groaned, a primitive expression of anguish, and released her, stepping away, unable to look into her eyes.

"I'm sorry, Janie."

He left her standing there, too shocked to react, and strode through the house.

He was in love with her, but he couldn't let her follow him from camp to camp, becoming a shadowy presence as his mother had in the rough-and-tumble life at construction sites.

A rash promise was now ruining his life. If he stayed in the States, he was honor-bound to follow in his grandfather's footsteps and take over the company. He knew deep down in the depths of his soul that would destroy him. How could his love for Jane overcome the resentment he'd feel?

After years of indifference to family ties, his one link to his mother was strangling him. The irony was that Rupert hadn't tried to forge any kind of personal relationship with him. This was just another business deal, a way for an old man to ensure that his life's work would remain tied to him by blood.

Luke went back to the pool and swam until his shoulders burned from exertion and his legs felt too heavy to keep moving. Then he sat naked on the concrete apron, shivering through the cool hours before dawn until the midnight blue of the late-night sky faded into daybreak.

## 11

JANE KNEW it was the end.

Luke must think she'd lost all self-respect when she agreed to trade her love for his cooperation, but her job had nothing to do with her decision. She'd been willing to make love with no strings attached or on any terms he wanted, but still he'd rejected her. She would never forget standing nearly naked and needy while he walked away.

At first she'd cried, but her pain was too great to be washed away by tears. In the morning she'd had no idea how long she'd slept. The whole night had been a series of awakenings, always with a sense of being crushed by loss.

The next morning Luke was gone, his bedroom door standing wide-open and his belongings cleared out. Seeing the empty room, the bed neatly made even though Mrs. Horning was still in Mesa, drained the last of Jane's hope. Chalk up one whopper in the failed-relationships department, she thought sorrowfully.

At least she knew what Rupert Cox could do with his job and his ridiculous assignments. She and Kim had survived the misery and devastation of losing their mother; they could certainly get through some downtime on the job scene.

One thing she did deserve: a decent recommendation. She wasn't going to trust Miss Polk on this. She was going to the top to make her case, and she knew exactly where to approach the formidable CEO.

A luncheon for company bigwigs was on the agenda for today in the company's boardroom. Luke wouldn't be there, but she would. It was probably her last chance to tell her side of the story before she was booted out of her job. Rupert owed her a good recommendation; she wasn't going job hunting with a big black mark on her record, not after trying so hard to whip his grandson into what he perceived to be the ideal corporate image.

Attempting to mold Luke into something he could never be had been wrong from the beginning, and she should have had the guts to stand up to her boss much sooner. Her judgment had been clouded by love; she'd been willing to go along with anything to stay near Luke. Not to mention her obligation to support Kim.

She packed quickly, sick with dread at the prospect of facing Rupert, but absolutely determined not to slink away without protecting her job potential. That was Luke's style, not hers. He tried to solve his problems by disappearing whenever he didn't like a situation. Someone had to stand up to his grandfather, and she was the only candidate.

She drove to Phoenix and went right to the company, her empty stomach painfully knotted and her mind buzzing with the things she wanted to say to her manipulative boss.

She couldn't get to the boardroom without walking past the fountain. The sun shimmered on the cascading spray, and for one heart-stopping moment she saw a mirage of Luke standing under it. Then her eyes focused on the water, and her pulse slowed to normal. She was through with fairy-tale romance. It was time to look out for her own interests, and she could do it. All she had to do was present her case to the big boss and leave with her dignity intact, even if he told her to clean out her desk immediately.

The double doors to the inner sanctum of the movers and shakers were wide-open, and Jane could hear the buzz of conversation. Stepping with much trepidation into the unusually crowded room, she saw beyond the long, narrow meeting table that dominated the room to a side table set up as a buffet.

''Jane, here you are! Glad to see you.'' Rupert was beaming ear to ear, and he took her arm and led her into the room.

A cordial Rupert Cox was a surprise; a freshly shaved and shorn Luke, resplendent in a conservative pinstripe suit and burgundy silk tie, was a shock. He stood only a few feet away, charming a group of board members.

She stared, flabbergasted. He was articulate; he was gracious. Heaven help her, he was gorgeous. He was talking business as though the company was his life's work, his passion. Just when she thought the wild man had handed her one awful, final jolt, he was behaving like a to-the-manor-born CEO prospect. What exactly was he doing? And why? Why?

The current chief executive officer himself ushered her over to the buffet, a spread with enough platters and bowls of food for a catered wedding reception. She filled a plate as her boss urged her to try different items, but a few nibbles told her she wasn't up to food. As soon as he was distracted by one of his minions, she handed her plate off to one of the servers.

She wasn't going to get to say her piece to Rupert, not while he was working the room. Luke was avoiding her, not even looking in her direction, which was just as well. She was dying to know what he was pulling this time, but too afraid to confront him. The memory of their near-torrid night was branded on her consciousness; the pain of his rejection was like an open wound. She refused to nurture even the slightest hope that they might have a future together.

Illogically, she was sorry he'd finally gotten a real haircut. His hair still curled over his shirt collar, a lot longer than the current corporate norm but short enough to make him almost unrecognizable as the "homeless" man who'd crashed the party the previous evening.

He was up to something. Suspicion and curiosity kept her in the room even though her instinct for self-preservation urged her to flee.

She talked to people but only saw their mouths moving. It was impossible to concentrate on the words. Miss Polk even came over and congratulated her. Jane's stock seemed to be high; she felt as if she'd just been voted into an exclusive club, but it was one she didn't want to join. Finally she eased her way toward the doors, poised for flight.

And nearly collided with Luke as she started to race-walk down the corridor and away from the luncheon crowd.

"What do you think you're doing?" she asked in an angry but unplanned outburst as he blocked her way.

"Isn't this what you wanted?" he coolly asked.

"You're triumphant. You've tamed the savage beast and transformed him into a button-down-collar management type."

"It's not what I want, and neither do you. How did you pull this off, and why did you bother?" She gestured in the general direction of his stark-white shirt and elegant tie, but also meant his whole young-executive act.

"I'm only going along with the program. It's what you and Rupert both want, isn't it?"

His eyes, dark blue and searching, examined her face with such intensity she was forced to look down at his black wingtips, so different from the scruffy hiking boots he liked to wear.

"Your grandfather was ready to strangle you after your behavior last night, and I don't blame him. How did you explain coming in like a desert rat?"

"I told him it was a joke that backfired. And don't avoid looking at me, Janie. You helped to dress me for the occasion right down to my skin."

She wouldn't ask. She wouldn't even think about his cute round bottom and other spectacular attributes encased in the chaste white underpants she'd ordered for him. Whatever his game, he was playing dirty. She knew he was trying to get even with her for being another of his grandfather's flunkies. In a way, she didn't blame him, but it still hurt.

"Your grandfather is too smart to buy that it was a prank." Jane was incredulous. "The man is a captain of industry, and you want me to believe he fell for a phony story like that?"

"Sometimes people believe what they want to hear," he said dryly. "And sometimes they don't."

What had she said to him last night? Did she say

or do anything to reveal how much she loved him? She felt as though she was standing nearly naked in front of him again, only this time her emotions were being scrutinized, not her body.

"Are you really going to take over the company?" she asked as a smoke screen to avoid saying something she might later regret.

She had to start thinking of him as just another man-who-got-away, but forgetting him was going to be the hardest thing she'd ever done.

"If it's in the newspaper, it must be true," he said sarcastically.

"I didn't see the paper. Rupert really did release the news without your consent?"

"Or the board's. For some reason he let it slip past him, but says it wasn't intended for publication yet. His theory is that an insider doesn't want me as CEO, so the story was leaked to prejudice my chances. I don't know who I have to thank for jumping the gun."

"So you will take over. Did you plan to do it all along?"

He'd betrayed himself, and somehow that seemed even worse than rejecting her.

"I haven't lied about how I feel about desk jobs."

"You don't have to explain yourself to me," she said. "It's not my concern."

"I'm still leaving."

"Then why are you here?" She gestured at the boardroom, a beehive of activity at the end of the corridor.

"I wanted to be sure your future is secure."

"*My* future?"

Her future without him could only be bleak.

"You did your job well," he said without warmth. "You tamed me."

"Tamed." She repeated the word with silent anguish.

"Here you two are!" Rupert's voice boomed in the high-ceilinged corridor, and he was bearing down on them with a couple of minions in his wake. "Jane, I can't tell you how pleased I am. I couldn't have picked a better tutor for my grandson."

She could only stare at him in puzzlement and dumb misery.

"There will be a nice bonus for you, and you've earned a promotion. I'll let Miss Polk give you the particulars, but you won't be disappointed. Good work, Jane."

He patted her on the shoulder while Luke looked on with a scornful expression.

"Thank you, Mr. Cox, but I'm resigning."

No one was more surprised than she was, but she'd already made up her mind, and leaving the company still seemed her only option. She hadn't tamed Luke. She'd never wanted to change anything about him. All she'd done was try to carry out ill-conceived orders from Miss Polk to keep a job that had gone horribly wrong.

"You don't need to do that, Jane." Luke was the first to object.

"Yes, I'm afraid I do."

She'd made an unprofessional and unendurable mistake: she'd fallen in love with the boss's grandson.

She left, her heels echoing on the terrazzo floor. No one tried to stop her.

LUKE STOOD in a daze, watching Jane walk away. He felt as though he'd been hit in the midsection by a wrecking ball.

"What got into her?" his grandfather asked in a surprised tone that didn't demand an answer.

Luke didn't have one.

She was out of sight now, but the soft *tap-tap* of her heels still echoed in his head. He could hardly believe that only last night she'd been willing to make love with him for the sake of her career, and now she'd walked away from a promotion.

It had also been her submissiveness that he hadn't been able to handle. His ego didn't demand that she throw herself at him like a love-crazed teenager, but he wanted—needed—to have their lovemaking satisfy something more than his sex drive. He wanted to make love to her because he—

Luke realized his grandfather was watching him with a shrewd expression.

"She's quite a gal," Rupert said blandly.

"I guess," Luke agreed, angry at the older man for using Jane the way he had.

"Great legs."

Luke didn't want to discuss Jane's attributes with the man who'd used her as bait to lure him into the company.

"You and I have to talk," Luke said grimly.

JANE DIDN'T GO right home after quitting her job. She didn't want to face Kim until she could give her sister a good explanation about why she threw away her career, her promotion and probably her bonus. She especially didn't want to explain about Luke. The pain was so fresh and searing, she couldn't bear to tell her sister how Luke had rejected her. The situation would have been laughable if it hadn't hurt so much—both of them turned on, ready to do the deed, then he'd looked her over in all her semi-naked splendor and left.

Her eyes still clouded thinking about it. If she told Kim, she might bawl; sympathy would be her undoing.

"Jane, grow up!" she told herself bitterly. Happy endings were for storybooks. She had to focus on survival. Kim couldn't work on crutches, and the rent would come due just as it always did.

She drove around until it occurred to her she'd better save gas for getting to job interviews. Then she walked through a mall, but there was nothing in the stores to distract her, especially since even a new tube of lipstick was not in her budget at the moment. She had friends who found solace in whipping out a credit card and treating themselves to pretty things, but Jane was too practical for that kind of self-indulgence.

Finally she went home, and for the next two days pored over help wanted ads. Kim was unusually sensitive, not asking her questions or offering advice. It helped that she was still infatuated with her solicitous doctor, and Jane was glad. Kim was all grown-up and deserved a good relationship with a wonderful man.

As a stopgap measure, Jane signed up to do temp work, and there was a chance she'd get called to work a few days the following week. Somehow she and Kim would survive financially, but Jane knew her emotional recovery was a long way off. She'd fulfilled an impossible assignment, taming Luke, but it had cost her a job and her heart.

Two nights later she was working on a résumé, knowing nothing she wrote on it would help her get a good permanent position unless her former employer gave her a satisfactory reference. She dreaded talking to Miss Polk and hadn't done anything about asking for a letter of recommendation or cleaning out her desk.

Kim was out with her M.D. when the phone rang. Too lethargic to talk to anyone, Jane let the machine take a message.

"Jane, this is Luke Stanton."

As if she knew a dozen Lukes! But what had happened to Stanton-Azrat?

"When you get home," he continued in his machine-distorted, accented voice, "give me a call at 555-0729. Thanks, love."

She hated it when he used the word *love* without meaning the kind of love where people cared about each other and didn't hurt them.

"Oh, damn, damn, damn!" she said, erasing the message so Kim wouldn't hear it and decide to start giving advice to the lovelorn.

Jane had no intention of calling him, but his phone number kept running through her mind: 555-0729, 0729, 729, 29, 9. Where was he staying? Silly question. Probably at one of his grandfather's palatial homes.

Had he planned to step into his grandfather's shoes from the beginning? Was all his reluctance just a ploy to get better terms from Rupert? She didn't know what to think anymore. Whenever she thought about Luke—which was most of the time—she had trouble getting past the big scene: him naked and aroused; her pathetically eager; his abrupt change of heart. Humiliation had new meaning.

The next evening her born-again-virgin friends went to a movie to check out a new heartthrob who was collecting rave reviews. Jane went along, feeling a tad guilty about spending the money but reluctant to sit home wondering if Luke would call again. The exciting new star was a pallid blonde too young to be interesting to her. In fact, she was afraid no man, on celluloid or in person, would ever appeal to her after knowing Luke. *Charisma* wasn't just a word to her anymore.

Jane suspected the instant she got home that something was up. Kim had a coy, all-knowing expression that suggested she was in the mood to play mind games.

"Have a nice time?" Kim began innocently enough.

"The movie wasn't bad," Jane said evasively. "What have you been doing?"

"Oh, I read a couple of chapters for class. Being on crutches should be good for my grades. Also the phone rang so many times the receiver got hot."

"You're a popular girl," Jane said dryly, sure now that Kim was stringing her along.

"Oh, by the way, Luke called. He really wants you to call him back."

Jane didn't like the way her pulse started racing; she hated being aware of her own heartbeat.

"I don't think so," she said more to herself than Kim.

"You have to call him!"

Kim hopped on one foot over to the phone where

it lay on an end table and held the receiver out to her.

"Wouldn't it be easier to use your crutches?" Jane asked in the stern big-sister-knows-best voice she knew irritated her sister, hoping to defuse her determination that she call Luke.

"Call him, Jane. He's really eager to talk to you. Please?"

Instead of taking the phone, Jane walked into her room and left Kim holding it. Sure, Luke wanted to talk to her. He probably wanted to make some inane apology that would quiet his conscience and make her feel even worse than she did now. Or he wanted to say goodbye and wish her a nice life. She couldn't bear to hear that.

"Not on my nickel," Jane said, deciding she wouldn't talk to him no matter how insistent he was.

Unfortunately she did have a few things to pick up at the company, especially a picture of her mother and a cut-glass vase that had been her great-grandmother's, but she kept putting it off. Confronting Miss Polk would be bad enough, but how could she be sure Luke wouldn't be there? She couldn't imagine anything more awkward than running in to him at the office.

By Monday of the next week she had two job interviews scheduled for Thursday and Friday, but the temp job hadn't materialized. She was still on the list, but they didn't need her yet.

She came home in the late afternoon with three more job applications to fill out and barely enough energy to toss them on the kitchen table.

"You have a message," Kim said, zipping into the room, making crutches look like fun.

Jane held her breath, telling herself she didn't want it to be from Luke again but desperate to have some connection with him. She felt like half a person, functioning on the outside but numb inside.

"Miss Polk wants you to clean out your desk."

"I suppose I should go over there some day this week," she said without much enthusiasm.

"Not some day. Right away," Kim said sympathetically. "They've hired your replacement, and they'd like to have you do it this evening around ten. The security guard will take you up to the office."

"Why so late?" Jane asked, secretly relieved that she'd be able to go into the building at a time when she wouldn't meet anyone, especially not Luke.

"Mr. Cox has some ultraconfidential overseas conference call this evening. He doesn't want anyone in the office until he's finished," Kim explained, standing on one foot in front of the fridge and studying the contents as though she expected to find hidden treasure.

"Far be it from me to disturb him," Jane said bitterly. "He's only my own personal version of a natural disaster."

She hoped for the sake of her replacement that Rupert Cox didn't have any more sinfully sexy long-lost grandsons.

# *12*

THE WALKWAY from the employees' parking lot to the administration building was well lit at night, the pinkish glow making it a bit eerie as Jane hurried toward her old workplace at exactly 10:00 p.m. She didn't mind being on the spacious grounds after dark, knowing security guards were on duty, but the area around the fountain made her uneasy. She approached it with trepidation, remembering this was where it had all begun.

Shadows played across the illuminated display, the water cascading upward day and night to dazzle any passersby who otherwise might not be impressed by the Cox complex. She supposed it was a kind of advertising statement, the same water endlessly recycled in a city that had blossomed in the desert.

Her eyes started playing tricks on her again. She caught a glimpse of movement, probably only the play of light on the spray. Still it gave her pause. A vagrant could be on the grounds, and she didn't know how far away the closest security guard was.

Should she run to her car? She hadn't bothered to change out of her casual white shorts, tank top and sandals, so she didn't have the disadvantage of heels and a skirt if someone chased her. Still, she was no sprinter; her best bet if threatened was probably a good ear-splitting scream. Should she keep heading toward the office complex or retreat while she could?

She would love to forget the whole thing, but the guard in the main lobby was expecting her. It would be cowardly to abandon her possessions, especially a photograph that meant so much to her, and she very much wanted to put everything about the Cox Corporation behind her.

She'd brought a canvas bag to carry her things. She slipped her purse into it, giving it some weight in case she had to use it to defend herself, although she didn't suppose it would do more than momentarily startle an attacker. She moved forward slowly, eyes riveted on the pool, ready to scream and flee if someone was hiding in it. Much as she'd like to turn tail and run, she didn't want to be embarrassed by a second request to clear her desk.

Imagination had nothing to do with what she suddenly saw. What on earth was Luke doing in the fountain?

She had a split second to make her decision: dash away to the parking lot, streak toward the building or confront him. This time the Greek god under the spray seemed to be fully clothed, at least by his standards. He was wearing dress slacks and one of his new, fine, white cotton shirts open at the throat, both sticking wetly to his torso.

"What on earth are you doing in there with your good clothes on?" she asked, incapable of walking past without satisfying her curiosity.

"Keeping cool while I wait for you."

"For me?" This was too much. "You can't be."

"I am."

He stood as still as a statue, water still raining down on him.

"I'm only here to clean out my desk."

Not, she thought, to frolic with a wild madman in her ex-boss's fountain.

"Miss Polk's orders," she added to give weight to her mission, not that she felt capable of putting one foot in front of the other under Luke's scrutiny.

"I doubt that," he said, walking out from under the spray but making no move to wring out his streaming hair or brush the water from his strong, handsome face. "Miss Polk is on her honeymoon."

"Honeymoon? That can't be—I mean, she called and left a message. I never dreamed—who did she marry? When—"

"She and my grandfather had a simple civil ceremony this afternoon. They're on their way to Paris for a few days."

"Miss Polk married to Mr. Cox?" She was so bemused, for a moment she almost forgot why she was there—but not for long.

"If Miss Polk didn't call me to come clear my desk, who did?"

"It didn't look like you were going to accept or return any of my calls, so I persuaded Kim to arrange for you to come here."

How could her own sister be so underhand? Of all the tricks Kim had ever pulled, this was the lowest.

"She had no right—"

"Don't blame your sister. I badly need to talk to you," he said in a quiet voice that sent shivers down her spine.

"I hope the guard will let me in," she said. "Now that I'm here, I really do need to pick up my things."

She was trying to ignore the pathetic way he was standing in ankle-deep water, looking half-drowned in what had been nice clothes. If he wanted to play jungle boy, his act was much better when he wore a loincloth—or whatever he called that little black pouch that barely covered his...

"You may not want to pack up your things yet," he said.

"Of course I do."

She kept telling her feet to move, but they seemed to have taken root on the pavement.

"I meant it when I resigned," she said emphatically.

"There may be a nice position for you after the corporate restructuring," he said, taking a few steps closer until he was on the verge of stepping out of the pool of water surrounding the fountain.

"What restructuring?" she asked without enthusiasm, not wanting to hear that Luke had buckled under and accepted the job as CEO.

Or worse, that he'd deceived her from the beginning and had always intended to go along with his grandfather. If that were true, she'd made another horrible mistake about the character of a man, her worst ever because she might never get over Luke.

"Come on in and cool off," he invited her with outstretched arms. "I'll tell you all about it."

"No way. You come out here if you want to talk. You're ruining your new pants." She instinctively backed away, mistrusting herself, not Luke, if he came too close.

"I won't be needing them."

He stepped onto the rim of the pool, his bare feet making a little swishing noise.

"That must mean you're going back to Africa." Her throat was tight, but she couldn't let him know how she felt. Not when she knew he didn't feel the same way.

It didn't matter whether he took over his grandfather's job or hightailed it back to the bush. Either way, he was out of her life, so why did it hurt so much to know she was going to hear his decision now.

"Janie, love."

He'd never said her name that way, never called her "love" with so much warmth and longing.

He stepped down on the pavement and moved closer, letting her see that his rugged features were softened by passion. It was a look that didn't require words, but she didn't know what to make of it.

"You're…" She meant to say "really wet," but it was the moment for truth. "…the most special person I've ever known."

"I need you, Jane."

He took her in his arms, sighing deeply before his lips brushed tenderly against hers. His kiss was so sweet and satisfying, she lost herself in it, wanting it to last forever. She could feel the tickle of his breath on her cheek and hear the sensual murmur that welled up in his throat. The world around them ceased to exist as he dominated her senses and filled her heart with longing. She relaxed as he stroked her back and teased her lips apart with the tip of his tongue.

She loved the taste of his mouth, the texture of his tongue, the heady pleasure of being desired. She loved him.

He buried his hands in her hair, holding her head

while he nuzzled her nose and ear, his lips so gentle they tickled.

"We can't do this," he whispered.

She stiffened and pulled away, horrified by the possibility of another rejection.

"Jane—"

"You're a beast!"

She pushed hard against his chest with both hands, but moved him less than half a step.

"Go away! Never come near me again!"

"Janie!"

He caught her wrists, shackling them as surely as if he'd used handcuffs.

"Let me go, Azrat! I don't know what your game is, but I won't play it again!"

She struggled, but his grip remained firm without hurting her.

"You're angry because I left you that night."

He sounded calm and reasonable. That only made her more angry.

"I'm furious because you're an egotistical tease!"

"A tease?"

He did something too outrageous to be believed. He laughed.

"Janie, I didn't make love to you then because I was afraid I'd hurt you by going back to Africa. You have no idea how I hated walking away from you. You'll never guess how painful it was for me to want you like crazy and not be able to offer you a decent life without compromising everything I am."

"Right! And you're only being kind by doing it to me again!"

"I was trying to tell you we can't do what I want to do standing on the pavement under the lights."

He released her wrists and lifted one to his lips, softly kissing it.

"You tried to tell me that?"

Her anger and indignation drained, leaving her shaky and unsure. Blood was still pounding in her ears, and the area south of her navel was throbbing like an all-drum orchestra.

"I'm afraid you didn't quite succeed in civilizing me, darling, but I'm not an exhibitionist when it comes to making love."

In one quick movement he leaned down, grabbed her around the thighs and slung her over his shoulder.

"Put me down! Luke, put me down right now!"

She grabbed the tail of his shirt and hung on for dear life. If this was how a wild man treated his woman, she didn't know what to make of it. She was breathless with excitement.

"Put me down right now!"

His only response was a soft grunt.

"I'll scream! The security guards will hear!" She flailed at his back to no avail.

"I took care of them," he said smugly, if a bit breathlessly, taking quick strides toward the shadowy concealment between two rows of dark shrubs.

He lowered her feet to the ground with a relieved "oomph," and she lost her will to resist when he took her in his arms.

"I won't be a fool and let you go again," he said softly, shushing her with deep, hard kisses.

She caught her foot on something soft and tripped against him, all resistance to anything he wanted totally gone.

"My sleeping bag," he explained, going down on his knees and pulling her with him.

"You put it here! Why were you so sure I'd come?"

"I invoked the name of Miss Polk. How could you not obey?"

"She's not my boss anymore."

"Would you have come if your sister had told you I'd be waiting under the fountain?"

A kiss was her only answer.

His hair was damp but drying quickly, as all things did in Arizona's arid climate. She ran her fingers through it, combing the shortened strands with her fingers.

"I'm sorry you cut your hair."

"It will grow."

His voice was husky with passion, and she was afraid to believe this was happening.

But it was, and practical Jane was sent packing as Janie reached out for the buttons on his shirt.

Luke was edgy. Twice he'd come close to making love to Jane, and twice he'd backed away, hurting her and tormenting himself. He felt like a volcano about to erupt, but he wanted the night to be as memorable for her as it was sure to be for him.

Somehow, with fumbling on his part and nervous giggling on hers, they managed to strip off their clothes and hang them like stream-washed laundry on a bush. He zipped them into his worn but durable sleeping bag, not wanting little pests distracting them. He'd tried to think of everything: protection, warning away the security guards so she wouldn't be embarrassed, picking the only place of concealment on the grounds.

He knew what women liked; he'd had opportuni-

ties to learn. He just wasn't sure what would make
Jane happy, and nothing was more important to him.

"Luke."

She whispered his name, and his heart swelled
with love.

She was cradled against his chest, her tongue flick-
ing against his throat, then she wiggled lower and
caught his nipple between his teeth, teasing it while
one soft hand made lazy circles on his stomach, moving a little bit lower each time.

All the things he'd dreamed of doing during long,
restless nights alone were possible now, but the joy
of being with her overwhelmed him. It didn't matter
what they did together; it was what they meant to
each other that counted. He gently stroked her
breasts, so enchanted by the velvety smoothness and
the pebbly flesh surrounding her erect nipples that all
his urgency and apprehension was transformed into
a deeply pleasurable arousal.

"We have all night," he whispered in her ear.

"Unzip me, sir," she said, poking her hand out of
the sleeping bag to hunt for the zipper tab.

"Janie, you wouldn't...."

"Leave you? Not unless you're toying with my
affections. I only want to open this bag."

She took a bloody long time with the zipper,
kneeling, then leaning forward and crawling over his
feet to flatten it.

"There, isn't this nicer?"

She rose up on her knees and stretched languidly,
for one instant a temptress revealing her full breasts,
then a bashful lover linking her fingers to conceal
her femininity.

"Come here."

He half rose and patted the unfolded sleeping bag beside him, his voice sounding oddly muted in his own ears. "Please, Janie," he begged without shame.

She snuggled beside him, her left leg lying across his right, her hand resting between them.

His arsenal of sensual tricks had always seemed more than adequate, but how could he possibly please this woman as much as she deserved? He wanted her to melt with longing and climax repeatedly until she experienced all that he was feeling for her.

"Aren't you going to kiss me?" she asked shyly.

"You can count on it, love."

He kissed her softly at first then heatedly, filling her mouth with his tongue until her breath was as ragged as his. Straddling her hips, he lavished kisses on her shoulders, her breasts and the length of her torso, nuzzling her, his tongue finding her moistness.

"Now," she gasped, touching him with magical fingers.

Trembling with urgency, he held back, taking precautions, loving her with his whole being, joining his body to hers.

"Janie, I love you," he whispered, his release more satisfying than he could have imagined.

Holding her close, he fell asleep.

JANE AWOKE SLOWLY in the first light of dawn, remembering she'd fallen asleep still linked to Luke. His hand was heavy on her breast, and even though nights were always cool in the desert climate, his flesh against hers was overheated in the confines of the sleeping bag. But small discomforts were overshadowed by total awareness of the man cradled against her. She reached across his hip and lovingly patted his round, firm backside, then tickled the little hollow at the end of his spine until he groaned with pleasure and threw his leg across hers, locking her even closer against him. He awoke slowly, too, kissing her in all the little places he'd overlooked the night before, then parted her thighs and caressed her with the tip of his finger until she squirmed with pleasure and invited him to say good morning in the nicest possible way.

"People will be coming to work," she said some time later, drowsy with contentment. "Someone might see us through an opening in the bushes."

He'd unzipped the sleeping bag and was lying spread-eagle with her tucked against his side, her head cradled on his chest.

"Toss me my clothes," he said lazily.

"You mean I should get up, risk being seen and deliver them to you?"

"Be nice if you did," he teased.

"Give me one reason why I should be the one to get them."

"You're my woman."

"I'm what?" She yanked a cluster of chest hairs hard enough to get his full attention.

"Ow! My woman—if you want the job."

"I don't remember applying."

She leaned over him on one elbow, secretly admiring his lean, tan, bristly cheeks, just fleshy enough to nip with her teeth. But she didn't want to start anything—and he looked ready for anything she might have in mind—until they settled a few things. Quite a few things. Maybe getting dressed wasn't such a bad idea.

"I'll get them," she said, "but don't read anything into it. I'm only doing it for modesty's sake."

"Understood." He grinned sheepishly. "I only asked so I could watch your bottom wiggle when you walk over there."

"You're terrible!"

She scampered over to the bush, feeling so self-conscious she wanted to break off a branch and play Eve to his Adam. Gathering his clothes first, she noticed his conservative cotton briefs were conspicuously absent. She made a bundle of his trousers and shirt, then hid his skimpy black pouch in one of the pockets, hurling the wadded-up garments directly at him. She dressed herself behind the thickest part of the bush, relieved when she was clothed.

"Your nice clothes are a mess," she said, turning around to find that he was dressed. "I think the pants shrunk."

"I won't need them," he said.

He was going back to Africa. She'd known since the beginning, but that didn't make it any less painful. A night like last night probably only happened to one woman in a million. How could she go back to an ordinary life without him?

"You're leaving."

"Yes, I have some things to take care of, but I'm coming back."

"Here?"

"Come sit by me."

"Tell me the coming-back part first."

He got to his feet in one fluid movement and took both her hands, standing in front of her with a boyish grin.

"I knew when you quit your job you were nuts—

or crazy about me—to put up with my antics for the sake of keeping it, then tossing it away, promotion and all.''

''I really needed the job, but I guess I needed you more.''

''Oh, love, when I realize I nearly blew this...''

He kissed her. Kissed her again. The morning sun was liquid gold around their tiny patch of shade, and someone called out to another person on the walkway beyond their hideaway.

''You can't be CEO of the company,'' she said with alarm. ''You'll hate it, Luke. And you can't break your promise to your grandfather, or you'll hate yourself.''

''Will you come with me to Africa?''

''Yes.''

It might not be right for her, but being separated from Luke would be so wrong.

''There are places I want to show you, people I want you to meet,'' he said with a dreamy expression on his face that made her insides feel like roasted marshmallows.

''I want to be part of your life no matter where you go, Luke.''

''Three or four weeks should be long enough. Do you want to get married here before we leave?''

''Married! Leave in three or four weeks?''

She had a funny, scared feeling, but Luke hugged her close and it went away.

''No, stay that long. I should be able to tie up all my business in that time.''

''You want to live here, then? Run the company?''

Relief mingled with a sick feeling for his sake. He was going to buckle under to his grandfather.

"Did I say that?"

He tilted her chin and smiled down on her, his sapphire blue eyes easily the most beautiful she'd ever seen.

"You promised your grandfather—"

"The trouble was," he said gravely, "I didn't like being blackmailed into staying. I wanted to get to know my only blood relative, but Rupert didn't seem to have any time for me. I was angry—mostly at myself for making that dumb promise to take over for him if I liked the States well enough to live here."

He stroked her hair, combing it with his fingers.

"I've never seen dark hair as fine as yours."

"Luke!"

She couldn't get mad at a man who made her feel like a goddess, but he was driving her crazy, leaking out bits of information instead of telling her the whole story.

"Sorry, love." He brushed a soft kiss on her cupid's bow and lovingly patted her backside. "I should tell you about my talk with Granddad."

"Please do."

"Here, sit down on the sleeping bag. I don't want anyone to see us before you hear the entire thing."

They sat side by side, the fingers of his left hand linked with her right.

"I had a long talk with Rupert."

Still, he hesitated.

"Yes, but what did you say?"

"I outlined some of the programs I plan to implement if I take over as CEO." He laughed softly. "I'm not one to run a sweatshop. I favor a relaxed workweek with flexible hours and on-site child care.

Also, company-sponsored wilderness retreats for employees, plus some production incentives like stock distributions.''

''He'll never agree to any of that.''

''No? You should have heard what he had to say about my ideas on product diversification. And you've already heard what I think of all the dead wood in the upper echelon.''

''What was his reaction?''

She was breathless in anticipation, wondering if Luke had toe marks on his backside from being booted out.

''He decided he's been a little hasty about his decision to retire.'' Luke smiled broadly. ''He isn't so sure I'm CEO material when he does step down.''

''I don't understand any of this.''

''We hashed things out bit by bit for several days. Turns out he wants his grandson in his life, and he thought the way to guarantee it was to hand over the company. Of course, he planned to stick around to give advice.''

''He was using the business to hide his feelings?''

''Yes, and I behaved like an idiot to keep him at arm's length. Seems he was afraid I'd bolt if he came on too strong as the repentant granddad. My mother ran away because he was too heavy-handed and demanding. He didn't want that to happen with me, so he thought the best way was to tie me to him through company responsibilities.''

''What about his sudden marriage to Miss Polk?''

Luke covered her knee with his hand, gently kneading but not answering.

''I know!'' she said, stopping his hand on its upward trip so he didn't distract her from getting the whole picture. "Your grandfather married his other candidate for CEO. If not his grandson, then his wife would be his logical replacement."

"She's been his mistress and right-hand assistant for years," Luke said sheepishly. "I should've tumbled to it when she went off on the haircut crusade. It was a wifely thing, not what an executive secretary would insist her boss's wayward grandson do."

"You two wasted a lot of years," Jane said with new compassion for grandson and grandfather. "What will you do now?"

"Now that I'm all 'civilized'?"

"That's doubtful, but I'm glad you're not at odds with your grandfather anymore. Even though he can be overbearing, I think he's just a lonely man who misses his family."

"Tell me, Janie love," he said, taking her hand in his. "Why did you stick with the job when I was doing my best to drive you away? I know your sister needs help from you, but there was something more, wasn't there? Do you love me the way I love you?"

"I guess the answer is yes."

"You guess!"

He tumbled her onto her back and hovered over her, his grinning lips only inches away.

"I'd have to hear exactly how much that is," she said.

"You're going to hear, again and again and again. Jane Grant, I love you immensely, immeasurably, unceasingly."

He proved it with a kiss that made her tingle all the way to her toes.

"I have a confession to make," he said in a soft

voice. "Actually I've fallen in love twice since I've been here."

"Twice?" She had a sudden fear that he wasn't kidding.

"First with you." He kissed her softly and reached under her rumpled tank top to caress her breast. "Then with this beautiful desert country of yours. When we get back from our honeymoon—"

"Honeymoon?"

"How do you feel about a safari after I've taken care of my business? Show you something of my world before I come live in yours."

"I can't believe this is happening!" Her happiness was bubbling up and almost overwhelming her. "What are you going to do when we come back here?"

"Make love to you, build bridges, make love to you—it would be nice to try a proper bed."

"What about your grandfather's company?"

"There may be a place for me someday in the corporate structure, but meanwhile..."

His kiss told her all she needed to know about "meanwhile."

# MILLS & BOON®

*Makes any time special*™

Copyright © Harlequin Enterprises Limited 1997
All rights reserved

**Mills & Boon publish 29 new titles every month. Select from...**

Modern Romance™          Tender Romance™

Sensual Romance™

Medical Romance™   Historical Romance™

MAT2

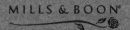

MILLS & BOON®

# Modern Romance™

**THE HUSBAND ASSIGNMENT** *by Helen Bianchin*

Career woman Stephanie Sommers's new assignment is
to set up a crucial business deal, not find a husband! But
she hasn't bargained on having to deal with gorgeous
Frenchman Raoul Lanier—or the instant sexual
attraction between them…

**THE PLAYBOY'S VIRGIN** *by Miranda Lee*

When brilliant advertising tycoon Harry Wilde helped
Tanya take charge of her recently inherited company,
he fell for her in no time at all! But Tanya had said she
wasn't the marrying kind…

**SECRET SEDUCTION** *by Susan Napier*

Nina had lost her memory, but it was clear that
stranger Ryan Flint recognised her. He seemed angry
with Nina, and yet intent on seducing her. When their
passion finally exploded what secrets would be
revealed?

**RHYS'S REDEMPTION** *by Anne McAllister*

Rhys Wolfe would never risk his heart again. He cared
about Mariah, but they were simply good friends. Their
one night of passion had been a mistake. Only now
Mariah was pregnant—and Rhys had just nine months
to learn to trust in love again!

## On sale 6th October 2000

*Available at most branches of WH Smith, Tesco,
Martins, Borders, Easons, Volume One/James Thin
and most good paperback bookshops* 0009/01a

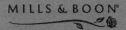

# Modern Romance™

**MISTRESS OF THE SHEIKH** by *Sandra Marton*
Sheikh Nicholas al Rashid is hailed in his homeland as the Lion of the Desert, and Amanda has been commissioned to refurbish his already luxurious Manhattan apartment. Just why does Nick seem so intent on making Amanda his mistress?

**THE BABY SCANDAL** by *Cathy Williams*
Ruth was stunned when her boss, Franco Leoni, took an interest in her. Franco didn't want a secret affair, but Ruth was afraid of scandal. Only there was one thing she couldn't hide: she was expecting his baby!

**A SPANISH REVENGE** by *Sara Wood*
Jude holds his ex-lover, Taz, and her father directly responsible for his father's loss of health. Taz is determined to stop Jude from carrying out his ultimate revenge plan—to marry her stepmother. If he marries anyone it should be *her*—and for love…

**MARRY IN HASTE** by *Moyra Tarling*
Evan Mathieson had once asked Jade to marry him—but now he proposed a different arrangement. He had suddenly become parent to his nephew Matthew, and had a fight on his hands to keep him. Evan needed a wife—and he wanted Jade!

## On sale 6th October 2000

*Available at most branches of WH Smith, Tesco, Martins, Borders, Easons, Volume One/James Thin and most good paperback bookshops*

0009/01b

For better, for worse... for ever

Brides and Grooms

Available at branches of WH Smith, Tesco, Martins, Borders, Easons,
Volume One/James Thin and most good paperback bookshops

# FREE
## 4 BOOKS
### AND A SURPRISE GIFT!

We would like to take this opportunity to thank you for reading this Mills & Boon® book by offering you the chance to take FOUR more specially selected titles from the Modern Romance™ series absolutely FREE! We're also making this offer to introduce you to the benefits of the Reader Service™—

- ★ FREE home delivery
- ★ FREE monthly Newsletter
- ★ FREE gifts and competitions
- ★ Exclusive Reader Service discounts
- ★ Books available before they're in the shops

Accepting these FREE books and gift places you under no obligation to buy; you may cancel at any time, even after receiving your free shipment. Simply complete your details below and return the entire page to the address below. **You don't even need a stamp!**

**YES!** Please send me 4 free Modern Romance™ books and a surprise gift. I understand that unless you hear from me, I will receive 6 superb new titles every month for just £2.40 each, postage and packing free. I am under no obligation to purchase any books and may cancel my subscription at any time. The free books and gift will be mine to keep in any case.

P0ZEC

Ms/Mrs/Miss/Mr ..................................................Initials ...............................................
                                                                                                 BLOCK CAPITALS PLEASE
Surname ..........................................................................................................................
Address ...........................................................................................................................

..........................................................................................................................

.............................................................Postcode ..............................................

**Send this whole page to:**
**UK: FREEPOST CN81, Croydon, CR9 3WZ**
**EIRE: PO Box 4546, Kilcock, County Kildare (stamp required)**

Offer valid in UK and Eire only and not available to current Reader Service subscribers to this series. We reserve the right to refuse an application and applicants must be aged 18 years or over. Only one application per household. Terms and prices subject to change without notice. Offer expires 31st March 2001. As a result of this application, you may receive further offers from Harlequin Mills & Boon Limited and other carefully selected companies. If you would prefer not to share in this opportunity please write to The Data Manager at the address above.

Mills & Boon® is a registered trademark owned by Harlequin Mills & Boon Limited.
Modern Romance™ is being used as a trademark.

Together for the first time
3 compelling novels by
bestselling author

# PENNY
# JORDAN

*The*
*Bride's*
BOUQUET

**One wedding — one bouquet —
leads to three trips to the altar**

*Published on 22nd September*

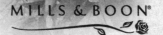

MILLS & BOON®

0010/116/MB6